P9-DWT-581

"Why did you run from me last night?" D.B. whispered.

Afraid her voice was going to fail her, Margo swallowed desperately. "I—I'm sorry about that. But I think we both know it would have been a mistake if I hadn't."

His hand reached up and closed gently around her throat. Margo began to tremble and she knew he could feel the telltale throb of her heart against his fingertips.

"A mistake?" he whispered, a crooked curve to his lips. "It didn't feel like a mistake when we kissed. Did it?"

No! It had been pure, sweet magic. And she'd never wanted it to stop. But to take up where they'd left off last night would be taking a step to ruination. D.B. only wanted sex. That was pretty obvious to Margo. And she? Well, she didn't want any man in her life— *especially* D.B....

Dear Reader,

Happy Valentine's Day! Love is in the air...and between every page of a Silhouette Romance novel. Treat yourself to six new stories guaranteed to remind you what Valentine's Day is all about....

In Liz Ireland's *The Birds and the Bees,* Kyle Weston could truly be a FABULOUS FATHER. That's why young Maggie Moore would do *anything* to reunite him with his past secret love—her mother, Mary.

You'll find romance and adventure in Joleen Daniels's latest book, *Jilted!* Kidnapped at the altar, Jenny Landon is forced to choose between the man she truly loves— and the man she *must* marry.

The legacy of SMYTHESHIRE, MASSACHUSETTS continues in Elizabeth August's *The Seeker.*

Don't miss the battle of wills when a fast-talking lawyer tries to woo a sweet-tongued rancher back to civilization in Stella Bagwell's *Corporate Cowgirl.* Jodi O'Donnell takes us back to the small-town setting of her first novel in *The Farmer Takes a Wife.* And you'll be SPELLBOUND by Pat Montana's handsome— and magical—hero in this talented author's first novel, *One Unbelievable Man.*

Happy reading!

Anne Canadeo
Senior Editor

Please address questions and book requests to:
Reader Service
U.S.: P.O. Box 1325, Buffalo, NY 14269
Canadian: P.O. Box 1050, Niagara Falls, Ont. L2E 7G7

CORPORATE COWGIRL
Stella Bagwell

Silhouette
ROMANCE™
Published by Silhouette Books
America's Publisher of Contemporary Romance

If you purchased this book without a cover you should be aware
that this book is stolen property. It was reported as "unsold and
destroyed" to the publisher, and neither the author nor the
publisher has received any payment for this "stripped book."

To my husband,
who sometimes hangs up his spurs just for me

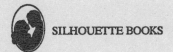 SILHOUETTE BOOKS

ISBN 0-373-08991-0

CORPORATE COWGIRL

Copyright © 1994 by Stella Bagwell

All rights reserved. Except for use in any review, the reproduction
or utilization of this work in whole or in part in any form by any
electronic, mechanical or other means, now known or hereafter
invented, including xerography, photocopying and recording, or in
any information storage or retrieval system, is forbidden without
the written permission of the editorial office, Silhouette Books,
300 East 42nd Street, New York, NY 10017 U.S.A.

All characters in this book have no existence outside the imagination of
the author and have no relation whatsoever to anyone bearing the same
name or names. They are not even distantly inspired by any individual
known or unknown to the author, and all incidents are pure invention.

This edition published by arrangement with Harlequin Enterprises B.V.

® and TM are trademarks of Harlequin Enterprises B.V., used under
license. Trademarks indicated with ® are registered in the United States
Patent and Trademark Office, the Canadian Trade Marks Office and in
other countries.

Printed in U.S.A.

Books by Stella Bagwell

Silhouette Romance

Golden Glory #469
Moonlight Bandit #485
A Mist on the Mountain #510
Madeleine's Song #543
The Outsider #560
The New Kid in Town #587
Cactus Rose #621
Hillbilly Heart #634
Teach Me #657
The White Night #674
No Horsing Around #699
That Southern Touch #723
Gentle as a Lamb #748
A Practical Man #789
Precious Pretender #812
Done to Perfection #836
Rodeo Rider #878
*Their First Thanksgiving #903
*The Best Christmas Ever #909
*New Year's Baby #915
Hero in Disguise #954
Corporate Cowgirl #991

*Heartland Holidays trilogy

STELLA BAGWELL

lives with her husband and teenage son in southeastern Oklahoma, where she says the weather is extreme and the people friendly. When she isn't writing romances, she enjoys horse racing and touring the countryside on a motorcycle.

Stella is very proud to know that she can give joy to others through her books. And now, thanks to the Oklahoma Library for the Blind in Oklahoma City, she is able to reach an even bigger audience. The library has transcribed her novels onto cassette tapes so that blind people across the state can also enjoy them.

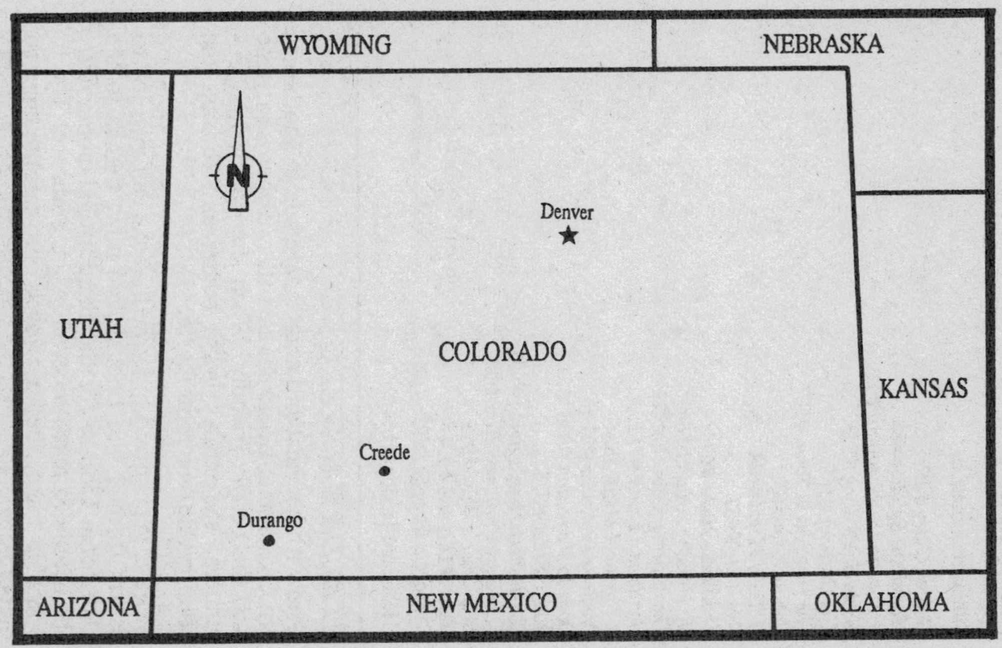
WYOMING
NEBRASKA
UTAH
N
Denver
COLORADO
KANSAS
Creede
Durango
ARIZONA
NEW MEXICO
OKLAHOMA

Chapter One

She was freezing to death! It was the end of June but Margo Kelsey couldn't imagine the dead of winter being any colder than this. The sun had long ago dipped behind the wall of the Rocky Mountains to her left and the night air rushed in around the windows of the Jeep.

It had been warm when she'd landed at the Durango airport, but now, after driving several hours north, the air had grown thin and cool. Since Margo was used to balmy Santa Monica, she'd expected Colorado to be cooler. She just hadn't expected it to feel like Siberia!

Thank goodness she was finally nearing the end of her journey. Or so Margo hoped she was nearing it. How could one be sure when the only road markings to be seen were cow droppings or an old dilapidated mining shack? If she drove much farther she figured she'd be totally off the map!

After another minute of bumping and lunging over the rough dirt road, the Jeep's headlights finally illuminated a group of buildings just ahead of her. This had to be the Silver Spur, she thought with a sigh of relief. Nothing other than a mountain dude ranch could be this far back from civilization.

Fifty yards passed before the Jeep rattled over a cattle guard. Leaning forward, Margo clutched the steering wheel and peered through the dusty windshield. Could this place actually be the Silver Spur?

Utterly shocked, Margo drove cautiously onward, past a row of small wooden cabins that didn't look much better than some of the mine shacks she'd seen on the way up here. This couldn't be right, she thought, her mind refusing to digest anything she was seeing.

When her boss, George Barlow, had asked her to go to the Silver Spur, she'd expected it to be a modern guest ranch with all the luxuries and facilities that went with any nice place of lodging. This place was primitive. It would do well to have the basic necessities! What had she gotten herself into?

D. B. Barlow heard the Jeep long before its headlights swept across that part of the ranch he could see from his bedroom window. He wasn't expecting anyone, especially not at this late hour. But sometimes, tourists going through to Lake City unfortunately got off on the wrong road and wound up here.

With a frustrated sigh, he threw back the covers and reached for his jeans and boots. More than likely the night traveler wouldn't leave until he went down and set them on the right track.

Out in the yard, Margo stopped her vehicle a few feet away from a log structure that appeared to be a scaled-down version of a lodge. Since there wasn't a sign pointing to an office, she could only guess that this was where the ranch guests checked in.

Stepping carefully down from the Jeep, she glanced around at the row of small cabins and a larger building just a few yards away from them. At the moment everything was in total darkness and she wondered if she'd made a wrong turn somewhere back near Wagon Wheel Gap.

A quick glance at her watch told her it was only a little past midnight. Could everyone around here already be in bed? Margo, who usually didn't start unwinding until this time of night, couldn't imagine going to bed this early.

Shivering and gritting her teeth to keep them from chattering, she reached inside the Jeep and pressed long and hard on the horn. If she woke anyone, she couldn't help it. She was cold, exhausted and hungry. She couldn't stay out here all night!

"There's no need to wake up the whole ranch."

The unexpected sound of a man's voice had Margo spinning around to see the orb of a flashlight coming straight at her.

"I—" She stopped, her eyes squinting as she tried to see the person she was talking to. "Sorry about that, but there didn't seem to be anyone rousing."

D.B. stepped closer and aimed the flashlight on the unexpected visitor. What he saw momentarily stunned him. This woman couldn't be much past twenty-five or twenty-six and dressed as if she'd just sauntered down Rodeo Drive. Never in his wildest imaginings would he have expected to find someone like her out in his ranch yard at midnight.

"Well, it's a damn cinch they are now, lady," he said, not bothering to hide his annoyance. "Do you know where you are? Are you having some sort of trouble?"

The only trouble Margo could see around here was him. Did he greet all the guests with this hateful, I-don't-want-to-be-bothered attitude?

Still trying to keep her teeth from knocking together, she said as primly as she could manage, "I think I'm on the Silver Spur Dude Ranch. At least that's where I was headed. Have I come to the right place?"

This woman, this blond glamour girl in her black high heels and white silk blouse was asking him if she'd come to the right place? It was all D.B. could do to keep from laughing in her face.

"This is the Silver Spur," he said. "But I think you've made a mistake. I'm not expecting any guest." And he sure as hell wouldn't be expecting one like her, he silently tacked on.

Margo's mouth fell open and she quickly stepped toward the flashlight and the unfriendly voice.

"Not expecting me! Are you D. B. Barlow?" she asked, frustration making the question sound more like a demand.

"In the flesh," he answered tersely. "Would it be asking too much for you to tell me who you are?"

The aim of his flashlight finally slipped away from her face, allowing Margo to get a look at him. The sight struck her like a thunderbolt.

This was D. B. Barlow? He looked like the perfect specimen for a cigarette ad, not a California CPA!

Wondering why she was shaking even harder than before, Margo thrust her hand toward the dark-haired man with the steely look in his eyes. "How do you do, Mr. Barlow. My name is Margo Kelsey. I'm your fa-

capable of tackling anything and succeeding at it, wanted to help him do just that.

"Like I said before, Ms. Kelsey, the best thing for you to do is hit the road back to California. And when you get there, tell my father not to send a woman to do a man's job."

Margo's teeth gnashed together, but this time it wasn't in an effort to keep them from chattering. No, the furthest thing she was feeling at the moment was cold. Blood was pumping furiously through her, staining her cheeks with heat and pounding like a drum at her temples.

Letting out a long breath, she carefully counted to ten before she spoke. "Perhaps you're right about Grace after all. The poor woman must be going off kilter. She told me you were a kind, fair man."

One corner of his mouth lifted in a sneerlike smile. "Grace always was misguided by good intentions."

Margo couldn't believe this man. It was no wonder George had given up trying to deal with him in the normal way a father might deal with a wayward son.

"Whether you want to hear about your father or not, I need a place to stay tonight." Margo didn't like pointing out her predicament to this man. Especially when he was the one who'd put her in it. But at the moment, she didn't have any other choice.

"All my cabins are full."

Margo's full lips compressed to a tight, thin line. "I wonder why I don't believe you."

He shrugged and even in the semidarkness, Margo had to appreciate his rugged fitness, the strong, handsome lines of his face.

"I don't care if you believe me or not. Go look for yourself. But be prepared. Most people don't like their sleep being disturbed in the middle of the night. Especially when they're on vacation."

On vacation...in this dump? What sane person would come here? Margo wanted to ask him. "Well, surely you have an extra room around here somewhere. A lobby with a couch?"

"This isn't a hotel."

"I can certainly see that."

Then why couldn't she see that she wasn't welcome? D.B. wondered. "You'd be doing yourself a favor to drive back down to Creede. Unless there's been an influx of tourists these past couple of weeks, you should be able to find overnight lodging there."

Drive back to Creede! She'd park herself on this man's doorstep before she drove back over the treacherous mountain road in the dark. "You might want me dead and out of your hair, but I'd just as soon not be. So if you can't find a place for me to sleep then I'll sleep here on the porch. Maybe in the morning when your guests find me here, they'll understand that you can't always be a gracious host."

A string of curse words lodged in D.B.'s throat as he struggled to keep from losing what little control he had over his temper.

"Go get your things. You can stay with me tonight."

Margo had the good sense to do as he said without putting up any more arguments. There'd be plenty of time later to let this man know what a number-one jerk he was. Tonight she was desperate for food and rest.

After she'd gotten her bags, D.B. took her into what she'd first thought had been a lodge. Yet as soon as she stepped inside and he switched on a floor lamp, she knew that this was his personal home.

A huge stone fireplace covered a large portion of one wall of the long living room. Without giving him the slightest glance, Margo hurried toward the low-burning flames and held her hands out toward the welcoming heat.

"Make yourself at home. I'm sure you will anyway," he said dryly.

Margo glanced up from the warm fire to see he was only a step or two away from her. And even though the room was dimly lit, the sight of him made her breath lodge in her throat.

This man couldn't have worked for years as an accountant. He looked the furthest thing from it. Besides the impression of being tough and brawny, D. B. Barlow was damn good-looking. His chocolate-brown eyes were fringed with the thickest, darkest lashes she'd ever seen. And that mouth... Just looking at it sent shivers down Margo's spine.

D.B. actually felt her gaze slide over his face, across his shoulders, then settle back on his mouth. The fact that she was looking at him in such a purely physical way affected him far more than he cared to admit. But a man would have to be dead not to be stirred by a young, beautiful woman.

And Margo Kelsey was a beautiful woman. There was no denying it, he admitted to himself as he continued to stare back at her. The streaks in her hair, which was bobbed at the top of her shoulders, ranged from a toffee color, to sand, then wheat and finally cotton. At the moment it hung straight from a side part and fell provocatively over her right eye. An eye too green to be turquoise and too blue to be aqua. Her eyes were the color of a soft blue Easter egg, and at the moment they held a look of anticipation that fired off all sorts of erotic images in his mind.

"Just tell me where to sleep and I'll not bother you anymore," she said, the directness of his gaze making her voice come out far softer and huskier than she'd meant it to be.

Not bother him? Like hell, D.B. thought. She was bothering him right now. She was reminding him that it had been a long time since he'd seen an attractive woman like her and even longer since he'd made love to one. But that was only a part of it. Ms. Margo Kelsey was a perfect picture of his past. A past he'd been desperately trying to forget.

"I'll be back in a minute," he muttered, then turned on his heel and left her.

Margo stared after him as he headed toward a staircase, then took the steps two at a time. Well, she thought, as he disappeared over the landing, at least she was in the house. That was better than where she'd been a few minutes ago.

While Margo waited for D.B. to return, she remained by the fireplace, soaking up the heat and taking a slow survey of the rustic furnishings of the room. Instead of chintz and ruffles, everything was made of either leather or wood. The polished pine floor had only one braided rug and she was standing on it. Over the mantel hung the mounted head of a beautiful antlered deer. Across the room, over a small rolltop desk was an enormous elk head.

It was definitely a man's house, Margo concluded. And one thing was for certain as she spotted D.B. descending the staircase: George Barlow's son was all man.

While D.B. had been upstairs putting on a shirt, he decided that making an issue over Margo Kelsey's arrival was the wrong thing to do. He wasn't going to let one little woman, who probably stood no taller than five foot four in her stocking feet turn him into a raging bear, or a rutting buck. He was going to show her that he could easily dismiss her or anything she had to say about his father.

Yet now as he looked at her huddled by the fire, her blond hair mussed, her blue eyes on him, expectant and waiting, he felt some of his resolve crumble like a piece of shortbread.

"There's a bedroom just through that far door," he told her, motioning with his head toward the opposite end of the room. "You can use it. There's a bathroom adjoining it, so you should have everything you need."

His clipped words had Margo wondering why he'd shown her the courtesy of putting a shirt on. He didn't seem to be concerned about showing her he possessed any other manners. "I know you're not particularly enjoying this, but—"

With a tight grimace on his face, he reached for her two leather bags. "You got that right, lady. And you might as well know right now that if you were a man, I'd have already kicked your butt off this ranch."

Margo's mouth fell open; then she hurried over to him, her high heels clicking furiously on the hard pine floor. When she was within inches of him, she stopped, tilted her head back so that she could see his face, then jabbed her index finger into the middle of his chest. "Then I won't tell you I'm grateful for the room—or your abominable hospitality," she said scathingly. "And as far as me needing to stay—"

Suddenly, and without warning, the room around her began to whirl and D.B.'s face was just a dim oval in the far distance. Before she realized what was happening, a weak moan slipped past her lips, then she tilted forward and straight into D.B.'s arms.

It was only a few seconds before Margo's equilibrium righted itself, but by then D.B. had a firm hold on her.

"Ms. Kelsey! Can you hear me? Are you going to faint?"

Margo's eyes fluttered open to find her head resting in the crook of his arm and his face hovering just above hers. Horrified at her own weakness and the fact that he'd been forced to hold her, Margo struggled to push herself away from him.

"I'm—all right," she spluttered. "You can let go now. I've never fainted in my life!"

In spite of who or what she was, D.B. discovered he was reluctant to release the grip he had on her arm and the back of her waist. The silk blouse she was wearing was as fine as angel hair and her soft flesh warmed his hands and invited him to explore what he could not see.

"Well, you were damn close to it for a minute or two. Are you sure you're all right?"

Margo thought she could hear actual concern in his voice, but in her disoriented state it was more than likely only wishful thinking.

"I—I'm okay now," she said quickly; then in a hurry to put some space between them, she stepped backward and immediately swayed like a drunkard.

D.B. grabbed her arm. "I think you'd better sit down."

Before she could protest, he led her over to a leather couch, then pushed her down on the buttery soft cushion. "What's the matter with you anyway? Are you pregnant?"

Outraged that he could ask her such a thing, Margo jumped to her feet, then paid for the sudden movement with another swirl of black in front of her eyes. Pressing her fist against her closed eyelids, she said in a tight little voice, "No. I am not pregnant! Not that it's any of your business," she tacked on as her strength began to return.

"I'd say it was my business since I'm the one standing around waiting to catch you," he said.

Margo took a couple of deep breaths before she lifted her head to look at him. What was he thinking? she wondered wildly. Did she look like a woman who slept around? For some insane reason she didn't want D. B. Barlow to have such a low opinion of her.

"I haven't eaten since early this morning," she explained. "And what with the long drive, I guess my body is telling me I need to eat and rest."

It was a damned shame how relieved he was that she wasn't pregnant—which didn't make much sense to D.B. He didn't even know this woman. It shouldn't matter to him if she was carrying some man's baby. But it did. He wanted to think of her as completely unattached and ripe for the taking.

Damn it all, D.B., have you lost your senses? a voice warned inside his head. This woman is bad news. She'll take you down in a hurry. Just like money-grubbing Roxanne took you down.

Frustrated with himself and with her, D.B. snatched a grip on her arm and led her toward the kitchen. "Didn't you have enough sense to stop and eat? Or does the old man keep you on such a rigid schedule you don't have time to eat?"

"If you're referring to your father, you couldn't be more wrong. George allows me to work at my own pace and do things as I see fit." Except for this little excursion, she thought wearily. She hadn't been too keen on coming up here when she knew there was bad blood between father and son. Family rifts were always bad news. But this whole thing was so important to George that she hadn't been able to refuse the older man.

"Then why didn't you take time to stop and eat? Anxious to see me?"

The mocking question made her grimace at him, even though she had to admit that a part of her had been curious as to what sort of man she'd find here on the Silver Spur. George had been a good friend and employer for three years now, and during that time he'd spoken often and longingly of D.B. Margo didn't know exactly what had happened to estrange the two men, but she'd come here with high expectations that D.B. would be a reasonable man. Boy, had those expectations been dashed, she thought.

"No, just anxious to get where I was going," she told him.

"Silly girl."

Margo wanted to remind him that she wasn't a girl, but with his fingers wrapped around her upper arm and his side brushing against hers, she didn't want him to get any ideas. The last thing she wanted to do was give him the impression that she was trying to seduce him.

Once they entered the kitchen, D.B. pushed her down on a stool beside a small breakfast bar. While he crossed to the refrigerator, Margo pulled off her high heels, let them drop to the floor, then wiggled to a more comfortable position on the small seat.

Dear Lord, she couldn't ever remember being this exhausted, and she didn't think it was all from the driving. No, the past half hour with D.B. had drained her far more than a whole day in court would have.

"Don't bother yourself," she said to him as he continued to dig in the refrigerator. "A wedge of cheese and an apple would be fine with me."

He glanced across the room to see that she was rubbing her bare feet. Her head was bent downward and her blond hair swayed against her cheek like a curtain in a gentle breeze. She didn't look like a lawyer to him. She looked like a woman of leisure, one who could do anything she wanted to do, buy anything that caught her eye and never have to worry if any of her choices were wrong.

"If that's the way you're used to eating, it's a wonder you made it here at all."

Glancing up, she saw him place a bowl of something in the microwave. "Don't tell me you're actually cooking something for me. I'm the enemy, remember? And if I hadn't been a woman, my butt would be somewhere over near Creede right about now."

Because his back was to her, she couldn't see the curve of amusement on his lips. "That's right. But I decided that a little thing like you can't be *that* much trouble. At least for one night." He switched on the microwave, then turned to meet her gaze head-on. "After all, you are leaving in the morning. And I think you know better than to ever come back."

He wasn't being sarcastic now, he was simply stating a fact. Still, Margo had to admit that it hurt her. His dislike for his father was spilling over onto her and she felt very saddened by that.

But she could never let him see her disappointment. She had to make him believe that she was a professional, a lawyer who looked at things coolly and deliberately and never let her emotions intrude upon her relationships with her clients.

Plastering a bright smile on her face, she said, "You've made your feelings quite clear, Mr. Barlow. And if I were you, I'd be more worried about my leaving than about my coming back. I can assure you that once I leave this godforsaken place, there won't be any danger in me coming back."

His expression was suddenly mocking. "What? Not your style? I'd have never guessed. I thought you'd planned on horseback riding in your alligator heels."

Margo started to ask him what he had against women who wore pumps, but at that moment the microwave chose to chime its bell.

He placed the bowl and a spoon on the bar in front of her. Margo quickly went to work on the contents, which looked and tasted like beef stew.

"I'm curious to know what made you want to be a lawyer," he said as he set a can of chilled soda by her bowl.

She swallowed down a bite of the stew and looked over to see him taking a seat on the bar stool next to hers. The closeness disquieted her—which was absurd. She was used to being near all sorts of men. At one time she'd even defended criminals. This man shouldn't strike fear in her. But he did. He stirred up a strange sort of reckless feeling in her. A feeling that she didn't want to analyze too much.

"So was my mother," Margo told him, a wry twist to her soft lips. "She couldn't understand why law should interest me. She thought I should be in a ballet troupe."

Margo laughed. "Poor thing. She never wanted to admit that I was too short, or that you have to have lots of money to study ballet."

"You have to have money to go through law school," he pointed out.

While sipping her cola, Margo looked at him from the corner of her eye. "I worked my way through."

D.B. was very surprised, though he tried not to show it. Margo Kelsey looked as if she'd been pampered since the very day she'd been born. Had he been wrong about her?

No, he wasn't going to soften his opinion of her just because she'd worked her way through law school, D.B. decided with grim determination. She worked for his father and that spoke volumes for D.B. She'd come up here to see him because George Barlow had paid her to. Obviously the old man was still trying to buy his love in God only knew what way.

"You sound very proud of yourself."

"Do I? I don't think so," she quipped, knowing full well he was simply trying to insult her. "Thousands of people have worked their way through college and law school. I'm just one of many."

D.B. knew the best thing he could do would be to leave the kitchen and let her finish the meal alone. Staying here and talking to her was only bound to encourage her. She might even get the impression that she could soften him up and talk him into contacting his father. And the idea of ever doing that was like swallowing a piece of twisted barbed wire.

Still, he couldn't quite make himself get up and say good-night to her. He told himself it was because he hadn't had any female company to speak of in a long time, and seeing this one with her lush little curves and soft blue eyes was a feast for his eyes, even if he didn't like what she represented.

Margo kept waiting for him to make another snide remark, but he remained silent, his brown eyes looking at her in a way that left her feeling like a defenseless little rabbit about to be preyed upon by a grizzly bear.

Shifting nervously on the seat, she spoke as casually as she could manage. "The ranch must be doing very well for you if all your cabins are full. Are you always this busy?"

When he didn't answer right away, Margo turned her attention back to her stew. She didn't want to give him the impression she was hanging on his every word. Being a lawyer, she was normally very good at getting all sorts of information from people. Yet she was also smart enough to know that D. B. Barlow wasn't born yesterday. He'd tell her only what he wanted her to know.

"Are you and my father wondering if the ranch is solvent?"

She looked over at him and suddenly she didn't know which infuriated her more, the sardonic twist to his lips, or his question. "You really are—"

He held up a hand to halt her. "No, don't bother answering the question. I'm sure George is wondering whether or not his son is in danger of going broke. What an embarrassment that would be for him if word ever got back to L.A. An investment tycoon with a son in the poorhouse. Bad advertisement, I'd say."

At that moment there were two things Margo would very much like to do to him: slap his face, and dump what stew she had left in the middle of his lap. Yet she could do neither. At least not if she expected to finish the job she'd come here to do. And because she hated like hell to fail at anything, she was even going to hold her tongue and not tell him what a verminous, hateful thing he was.

"Is that what you're trying to do? Is that why you bought this ranch—to embarrass your father?"

D.B. threw back his head and laughed long and hard. Margo could only stare at him and wonder how she could be so charmed by his tousled black hair, the way his white teeth glinted sexily against the tanned skin of his face and the way his brown eyes drooped to sleepy slits when he looked at her. All those things were purely physical, she told herself. The man had nothing on the inside except bitterness and cynicism. She was crazy to think there was even anything remotely attractive about him.

"Lady, I'm really beginning to feel sorry for you."

"My name isn't Lady," she reminded him through gritted teeth. "It's Margo."

Even though her voice sounded as though it were coming off chipped ice, there was enough fire in her eyes to set the whole San Juan forest ablaze.

Feeling the heat of her gaze and, oddly enough, liking it, D.B. grinned and slowly rose to his feet.

"Okay, Margo, why don't you tell me how often my father sends you off on these cockeyed missions? Do you do all of his dirty work for him?"

Her blue eyes continued to blaze back at him even though her heart was thudding with anticipation. "I've never encountered anything in my work that was dirty—until now, that is."

Chuckling smugly, he moved closer and curled his fingers around her wrist. "Well, who knows? You might find you like getting a little dirt under your fingernails. Why don't we find out?"

Before Margo realized what he intended to do, he'd taken both her hands and pulled them against his chest, deliberately resting her fingers against a patch of bare skin where his shirt hung open.

"You know," D.B. murmured huskily, "sometimes a little dirt is all it takes to make a thing grow."

In horrified fascination, she watched his face dip down toward hers. He couldn't be going to kiss her. He wouldn't dare! Yet the next instant he was doing just that, his lips shockingly tender on hers.

This wasn't the insulting thing she'd expected as he slid his arms around her and urged her closer. This kiss was a gentle invitation. One that Margo could not resist. And before she realized what she was doing, she was leaning into him, encouraging him to deepen the embrace.

"Hmm," he finally murmured, his finger tracing the puffy line of her lips. "You know, it's too bad you work for my father. Under different circumstances we might have liked each other."

Furious because she was afraid he might be halfway right, Margo jerked out of his arms. "Don't kid yourself," she spat; then, in a protective gesture, she pressed the back of her hand against her kissed, pink mouth.

"Well," he said with a shrug of his shoulder and a lopsided grin on his face, "since we won't be seeing each other after tonight, it hardly matters, does it?"

Still trying to pull herself together, Margo didn't realize he was leaving the room until she looked around to see him about to go out the door. "I don't intend to go anywhere until we talk," she warned him.

Pausing, he looked back at her. He could still taste her lips on his and the sweetness, he realized, had only whetted his appetite. "I thought we had been talking," he said.

Her gaze slid over his long muscled legs, his lean hips and broad shoulders. She'd never made love to a man like him, and God help her, she wasn't about to tangle herself up with this one.

"You might call that talking. I call it kissing," she pointed out.

He smiled with a cocksureness that made Margo's blood boil.

"Well, if that's what you're really wanting, I could probably summon up a little more energy tonight."

Margo's breast heaved as she tried to control her fury. "You don't really want to know why I came here, do you?"

The amused look on his face was suddenly replaced by a stoic mask. "Not in the least. So don't waste your effort on me."

She let out a short incredulous laugh before closing the few steps between them. "Oh, rest assured, D.B. I'm not doing this for you. I'm doing it for your father." She tilted her head back until her blue eyes clashed with his brown ones. "You see, he believes he's dying."

Chapter Two

D.B. stared at her as fear rushed to the pit of his stomach. What was this woman saying? His father couldn't be dying!

"My father was the picture of health the last time I saw him. How could he be dying?" he asked her.

Margo saw his face pale and knew this man wasn't nearly as indifferent to his father as he let on. The thought gave her a glimmer of hope.

"Correct me if I'm wrong, but you haven't seen your father in three years. A lot can change in that length of time."

His eyes narrowed as they searched her accusing face. "Are you telling me my father has a terminal illness?" he demanded.

Moistening her lips, she carefully chose her words. "No. I'm not telling you it's terminal."

D.B. grabbed her arm, but stopped himself short of giving her a shake. "Then what are you telling me?"

His fingers were like a hot vise around her arm. Margo wanted to shake them off, to show him that he couldn't intimidate her. But she didn't. His touch, the closeness of his body and the odd look in his eyes mesmerized her in such a way that she could hardly think, much less find the strength to get away from him.

"I'm telling you that I don't really know the severity of your father's health problem. Besides, he's the one you should be asking, not me."

He let out a long breath and released his hold on her arm. "I think I see now," he said in a soft, speculative voice. "That's what this is all about, isn't it? A ploy to make me get back in touch with my father."

Margo couldn't believe what he was saying. Was D.B. really that insensitive and heartless? Or was there actually another side of George that she'd never seen before? Could the man have done something to his son that went beyond forgiveness? Margo couldn't imagine it. In the past three years she'd known George Barlow, she'd seen nothing but a kind, gentle man. On the other hand, she'd known D.B. for less than an hour and had yet to see a shred of compassion in him.

Sadly, she shook her head. "There is no ploy. Your father has been ill. He truly believes he isn't going to live much longer."

"It's obvious that you think you know my father. But I can assure you that you don't. George Barlow will stop at nothing to get what he wants. And that includes putting on a dying act."

By now Margo shouldn't have been surprised by anything this man said. But she was. "I do know George. And I can assure you he isn't putting on a dying act. In fact, he's been working from his home for the last few weeks."

D.B. had to admit that sounded out of character for his father, a man who always wanted to be seen and heard. The offices of Barlow and Associates had always come before George's home life. Could Margo Kelsey be right? Could his father truly be that ill? One thing for certain, he wouldn't be suckered into going back to California simply on this woman's word.

"And I'm sure he wanted you to tell me all this," he said dryly.

She grimaced. "He doesn't want you to know he's been ill. But I thought you deserved to know the truth."

Oh, he'd find out the truth all right, D.B. thought. But not from her. "Did you now? I wonder why you'd want to be so straight with me? You don't even know me."

Margo was beginning to wonder why herself. The only thing this man really deserved was a swift kick in the butt.

"Believe what you want. It's obvious you're going to anyway."

"You're right about that," he said, his mouth twisting into a mocking little smile. "And now if you'll excuse me, I'm going to bed. I suggest you do the same. You've got a long drive ahead of you tomorrow."

"That's what you think," Margo muttered to herself as she watched him walk out the door. There was no way she was leaving this ranch until she'd had her say. And after tonight, that was going to be a hell of a lot!

When Margo woke the next morning, she felt as if she'd just closed her eyes—which probably wasn't too off the mark. Groaning, she groped for her watch on the nightstand. Six-thirty. The last time she'd looked it had read 3:20. Well, three hours' sleep was better than nothing. It had to be. She certainly couldn't stay in bed this morning.

Throwing back the covers, she sat on the side of the bed and rubbed her hands over her face. She didn't feel the least bit rested . . . thanks to D. B. Barlow.

The man had brought her blood to such a boiling point, it had taken her forever to unwind. And even when she had begun to relax, she still hadn't been able to get him out of her mind.

She'd never met such a macho, supercilious, hateful man in her life. Why George would *want* a son like D.B. back in his life was totally beyond her. Perhaps blood was thicker than water, as the old adage went, but in her opinion it would be better to let D.B. remain a black sheep and away from the fold. And it would definitely be better if she could go home and forget she'd ever met the man.

"An unexpected visitor arrived last night."

A tall, thin woman with bright red hair glanced over at D.B., then back to the griddle full of pancakes she was cooking. "Oh? I didn't hear a thing. Who was it? Forest rangers looking for somebody?"

"I wish," D.B. muttered.

The older woman cocked her head at him. "What did you say?"

"I said no. It wasn't rangers." D.B. got up from the worktable in the middle of the large kitchen and refilled his coffee cup. He came to the bunkhouse every morning at this time to drink coffee and visit with Wanda while she cooked breakfast for the guests. It was normally one of his favorite times of the day, but this morning he was definitely out of sorts.

"Well, are you going to make me ask twenty questions, or are you going to tell me who this unexpected visitor was?"

Wanda had worked for him since he'd first taken over the Silver Spur. She was an unpretentious, hardworking soul. D.B. admired her and considered her a good friend. He'd told her a little about the differences he'd had with his father, but not everything. In fact, no one on the ranch knew all that much about his past. They only knew he used to live on the California coast and that he'd been a rich, successful businessman.

"Her name is Margo Kelsey. She's from California."

"She? Who was she? A guest with her reservation dates mixed up?"

D.B. shook his head while vivid images of Margo filled his thoughts. He'd been around the woman for less than an hour last night, but he easily remembered everything about her. The soft huskiness to her voice, the infinite shades of blond in her hair, the blue of her eyes, the sweetness of her lips. Lips that he never should have kissed, he thought with self-disgust.

"No. She isn't a guest. She's my father's lawyer."

The metal spatula hovered over one of the browning pancakes as Wanda looked curiously at her boss. "Lawyer? What's the matter? Is someone suing you?"

Suing him? That thought had never occurred to him. But he supposed it could be true. Where his father was concerned, anything was possible. After years of watching George manipulate those around him, D.B. wouldn't put anything past the man.

"Not that I know of," he told her.

"You mean she didn't tell you what she was doing here?" Wanda asked, plainly bewildered by her boss's announcement.

D.B. moved over to the cabinet where a platter of bacon was being kept under a heat lamp. He took a slice and quickly ate half of it. "I wasn't particularly interested in what Ms. Kelsey had to say. I told her to leave."

Wanda's pencil-thin brows inched upward as she glanced at the dark scowl on D.B.'s face. "Did she leave?"

Grimacing, D.B. shook his head. "No. But she will later this morning. I'll see to it."

Wanda stacked the browned pancakes on a waiting platter and began pouring more batter onto the griddle. "Well, if she's still here, I'd better set a place for her breakfast."

D.B. let out a bark of laughter. "I wouldn't bother, Wanda. I doubt Ms. Kelsey will be able to drag herself out of bed for at least two more hours."

Margo hurriedly pulled on a fringed leather jacket and eyed herself critically in the mirror. Was she over-dressed? What did a person wear up here anyway? she wondered. Back in Santa Monica when she'd packed for this trip, she'd believed the Silver Spur would be a country-type resort with luxury rooms, spas and gyms, maybe a small golf course, and for those who wanted to play cowboy, a stable of thoroughbreds to ride on carefully manicured bridle paths.

How wrong could she have been! From the looks of things around here, her black ostrich boots were definitely out of place. But they were the only pair of cowboy boots she owned. As for her designer jeans and leather jacket, they looked far too new. But what did it matter? She wasn't here to impress D. B. Barlow with her fashion sense. She wasn't here to impress him in any sense. She was here to inform and persuade him, the latter of which she had major doubts about doing.

Downstairs, the house was quiet and D.B. was nowhere to be seen. Margo wasn't surprised. She hadn't really expected him to hang around and offer her breakfast.

Out on the long wooden porch, the morning was still chilly even though the sun had crested over the rise of mountains that curved around the eastern side of the ranch.

Hugging her arms against her to ward off the chill, Margo stepped down to the bare yard. She had no idea where D.B. might be this morning. The way her luck was going, he'd probably left the ranch entirely. But that wasn't going to stop her from looking.

With instinct guiding her, she crossed the ranch yard to the large log structure that stood about fifty yards away from the line of small cabins. Along the way, she carefully skirted piles of horse manure and loose rocks. However, there was little she could do to avoid the squishy mud that oozed up over the soles of the boots she'd paid a small fortune for.

The building turned out to be full of people, guests she supposed, who were all sitting down at long wooden tables. The smell of bacon and coffee permeated the air, reminding Margo she was ravenously hungry after her meager meal yesterday.

As the door shut behind her, it seemed as though every head in the room turned to look at her. Conversation and the clatter of cutlery came to an abrupt halt. Margo had stood in the middle of some tense boardrooms before, but she'd never felt as conspicuous as she did now.

Quickly she scanned the group of strange faces until finally across the far side of the room she saw a familiar dark head. At that very moment he looked around and her blue eyes clashed with his brooding gaze. Margo's heart jerked then took off in a mad gallop.

She couldn't believe she'd let *him* kiss her last night. Even worse, why had she responded to him in such a reckless way? She could only imagine what he was thinking of her. If the look on his face was anything to go by, he was probably listing her somewhere between trash and pond scum.

Oh, well, she thought, as she headed purposely toward D.B.'s table. She couldn't be worried about one little kiss, or his low opinion of her. The sooner she could talk to him and get this whole thing over with, the quicker she could go home. And for Margo that couldn't be fast enough.

A redheaded woman carrying a glass coffeepot intercepted Margo before she'd gotten halfway across the room.

"You must be Ms. Kelsey," she said to Margo. "I'm Wanda, the cook here on the ranch."

Apparently D.B. had already told this woman of her arrival, which only made Margo wonder what else he'd said.

"It's nice to meet you, Wanda. I'm Margo."

The cook's leathery skin wrinkled into a smile. "Well, Margo, you go have a seat and I'll bring you some breakfast."

Margo thanked her, then headed on toward D.B. who'd turned his attention back to his plate and the people around him. Thankfully there was an empty space on the wooden bench. Not waiting for an invitation, Margo slipped down beside him.

"Good morning, D.B."

He looked at her, his brown eyes making a slow perusal of her face. In spite of her late night, she looked surprisingly fresh, he decided. Her blond hair was pulled back into a ponytail at her nape and tied with a copper-colored scarf. Last night he hadn't realized how tanned she was, but now in the light of day her golden skin was a dark, warm contrast to her fair hair and eyes. She wasn't the most beautiful woman he'd ever seen, but she was certainly the sexiest.

"Good morning, Margo," he said slowly. "I'm surprised to see you here. I figured you'd either be asleep or gone by now."

She gave him the most dazzling smile she could muster. "And miss telling you goodbye? Never."

Stifling a groan, D.B. turned his attention back to the stack of pancakes on his plate. Across the table, two teenage boys, who looked to be identical twins, were both staring intently at Margo.

"Are you a new guest?"

Margo looked at the thin-faced teenager sporting a pair of thick, horn-rimmed glasses. "Uh, no," she said with a polite smile.

His twin quickly spoke up. "Are you lost?"

Margo wished she *was* lost. She wished this place wasn't really the Silver Spur and this dark-headed mountain man beside her wasn't George Barlow's son.

"No. I—"

"What an idiotic question, Willis! Does the woman look like she's lost?"

Willis glared at his brother Weston, then looked curiously from Margo to D.B. "Oh, I get it. You must be D.B.'s girlfriend."

D.B. was suddenly coughing. Beside him, Margo's face turned a bright pink.

"She isn't my girlfriend, boys. Her name is Margo and she's here—" D.B. paused long enough to give Margo a sardonic look "—on business."

She was here on business all right. And that business was between him and his father. She was just a go-between. A lawyer, trying to do her job. So it was silly, she scolded herself, to let the feel of his eyes on her make her heart pound like a drum.

"That's right," she murmured. "Business."

The twins began plying her with all sorts of questions. Before Margo could answer any of them, Wanda appeared at her shoulder with a plate of pancakes and a cup of steaming coffee.

Thankfully the interruption diverted the twins' attention to another guest at the table and Margo was able to focus on her breakfast and the best way to approach the man beside her.

After a few bites she said, "I hope that my news about your father's ill health didn't disturb your sleep last night."

Finished with his meal, D.B. pushed back his plate. Actually, Margo Kelsey and her news had disturbed him far more than he'd ever admit. He'd lain awake well into the morning hours, his thoughts alternating between her and his father. He still didn't know exactly what to think about this woman, or about his father.

With coffee cup in hand, he squared around on the bench so that he was facing her. "If you came all the way up here to tell me my father has been ill, then you've got the point across. You can go back to California and not feel guilty about the paycheck he'll give you."

Did he always bring everything down to money? she thought angrily. Or did he only do it with her? Careful not to let him see the flare of her temper, she said, "I don't think I've gotten the point across. Last night you told me you didn't believe me. You insinuated that your father was merely faking an illness to gain your sympathy."

D.B. suddenly couldn't look at her. Above anything he couldn't let this woman see or know just how much he still cared about his father. If she knew, she'd play on his feelings. And he wasn't about to let a woman or his father do that to him. Ever.

"If you must know, I was able to contact George's personal physician this morning."

"And?" Margo urged, surprised that he'd cared enough to look into the condition of his father's health. To her knowledge D.B. hadn't made any attempt to contact his father in the past three years. That didn't sound to Margo like a man who cared about anything but himself.

D.B. stared at the bottom of his coffee cup. "He told me that my father had suffered a minor heart attack about six weeks ago. However, he didn't give me the impression that my father was dying."

Margo let out a long breath as D.B.'s words pulled her back to the time George had been stricken with the attack. She'd been so terribly worried about him, not only about his physical health, but also the mental and emotional state he was in. The spell had frightened the older man and reminded him of his mortality. Once that had happened, mending the rift between him and his son had become an obsession with him.

"Tell me, D.B., could the doctor assure you that your father might not have a fatal attack in the coming months?"

He frowned at her. "Doctors aren't prophets, Margo. I doubt he could give you or I such a guarantee."

"Then you're not the least bit worried about him?"

D.B.'s expression was grim as he looked her in the eye. "Look, Margo, whatever you might think, I don't want my father to be either sick, or dead. I know he's getting good medical attention. So what do you want from me? If you're expecting me to lay out my personal life for you to examine, then you're crazy. What has or hasn't gone on between me and my father is none of your business. Got that?"

Margo looked around the table and was visibly relieved that the twins and the other guests had left. It was bad enough that he could speak to her this way in private. She certainly didn't want anyone else to hear it. "For your information, I don't want to know about the problems between you and your father! I've come here on other business. Business that is very pertinent to you. Or don't you care?"

He swung his legs out from under the table and in the process his thigh brushed against Margo's. She felt seared by the touch and her breath stayed lodged in her throat until he'd gotten to his feet and moved a few inches away from her.

Looking down at her, he answered. "No. I really don't care. I have a guest ranch to run. I don't have time for this."

Anger pushed her to her feet. "Then I suggest you make time," she said, her chin tilted haughtily up at him. "Otherwise, you're going to be seeing a lot more of me around here."

His brown eyes made a slow, insolent journey from the top of her head to the soles of her ostrich boots. "It's not the sight of you that bothers me, Margo Kelsey. It's your mouth that really gives me the problems."

More than anything, Margo wanted to fly at him with both fists. But she knew she couldn't. He'd never see her as a lawyer if she behaved like a hellion. Still, she had to do something to take the smug look off his face.

"Is that right?" she drawled. Her gaze deliberately settled on the tight line of his lips. "Well, I'm afraid it would take a lot more man than you to shut me up."

His brown eyes narrowed to dangerous slits and for a moment Margo was afraid he was going to ignore what guests remained in the bunkhouse and kiss her right then and there.

Margo let out a sigh of relief when someone behind them suddenly called out.

"D.B., are we still riding in an hour?"

D.B. twisted his head toward the man, whose rough work clothes made him look as if he might be a ranch hand instead of a guest.

"Right, Tom. I'll be down at the stables in five minutes," D.B. told him.

"What about me?" Margo asked when he turned back to her.

D.B.'s lips twisted into a mocking grin. "I don't think you want to hear what I'd like to do about you right now."

Her nostrils flared and heat filled her cheeks. "You're not a man," she said slowly. "You're a heathen."

D.B. laughed. "You see a man out of his suit and Italian shoes and you think he's uncivilized. Poor thing. You should get out more."

"I intend to get out—of here. Just as quickly as I can. But not until you've heard me out. Your father is making some changes in his life. You need to know about them."

D.B. hardly thought so. After all, he had his life here in the mountains, his father had his life in California. From past experience, D.B. knew it was better that way. The minute he tried to communicate with his father, trouble would start all over again.

Still, D.B. could see that Margo was a determined woman. The fact that she was still here on the ranch proved that. But maybe there was an easier way to get rid of her.

His expression suddenly thoughtful, he folded his arms across his chest. "You know, I'm beginning to wonder just how important this mission is to you."

Deliberately mimicking him, Margo folded her arms across her breasts. She corrected him. "It's not a mission, it's my job. And I take my job very seriously. If not, I would have kissed your sarcastic face goodbye a long time ago."

D.B. studied her flushed cheeks and flashing blue eyes and had to admit that this woman roused him like none he'd ever met. He didn't know why. And he damn sure didn't like it. But there didn't seem to be much he could do about it.

"Prove it to me."

Totally bewildered, she stared at him. "What?"

"The guests are going on a trail ride in less than an hour. If you go along, keep up and make it back to the ranch with the rest of the group, I'll give you thirty minutes to state your cause—whatever that might be."

Margo didn't know whether she wanted to curse him or kneel down and kiss his feet. On one hand she shouldn't have to prove anything to him. Yet on the other hand, he seemed to be offering her an olive branch of sorts.

She had to grab it, she quickly decided. For George's sake, she'd ride a horse. She'd even kiss its nose if it would make this man listen to her!

"You'll talk—"

"I'll listen," he interrupted. "Thirty minutes. Maybe thirty-five if you make it interesting."

Interesting? He was going to be bowled over with what she had to tell him!

"All right. I'll ride along," she agreed, then smiled at him. "And I'll keep up."

D.B. knew he was inviting trouble. The last thing he needed was a pampered city girl on a trail ride. Still, something inside him was prodding him, making him want to see just what Margo Kelsey was made of. And a small part of him, a part he wanted to ignore, actually wanted to know why she'd really come here to the ranch.

"You do know how to ride?" he asked her.

Ride? Margo had ridden motorcycles and surfboards with some of her past boyfriends. But not horses. When was the last time she'd ridden? she frantically asked herself. Summer camp after eighth grade? Oh, Lord, what was she getting herself into?

"Er, yes. It's been . . . awhile. But I've ridden before."

If D.B. saw terror in her eyes, he didn't let on. Instead, he merely said, "Good. Be down at the corrals in forty minutes. You might want a few extra minutes to get acquainted with your mount."

"Sure. I can't wait."

D.B. gave her a goading little smile, then turned and left the bunkhouse.

With a heavy sigh, Margo turned and retrieved her coffee cup from the table. What little there was left had gone cold, but she drank it anyway. She had a feeling she was going to need all the fortification she could get.

Chapter Three

"Grace, it's me, Margo. How are things there?"

"Margo!" the secretary shouted. "Where in the world are you? George and I have been worried sick when we didn't hear from you last night."

Passing a weary hand across her brow, Margo eased down on the rumpled bed she'd slept in overnight. "Sorry about that, Grace. I didn't get here to the ranch until midnight and then things—"

"You're at the ranch now?"

Grace made it sound as if Margo had managed to reach Venus instead of the Silver Spur Dude Ranch.

"Yes. But—"

"How is he? What did he say about his father?"

Because Margo adored the older woman, she rarely reminded Grace who was the boss and who was the secretary. But this morning her patience was rapidly wearing thin.

"Grace, D.B. said he never received my letter. Don't you find that a little odd?"

There was a pregnant pause, then Grace said, "Well, not when you consider that I didn't mail it."

Groaning, Margo's eyes lifted helplessly to the ceiling. "I hope you have a good explanation for this, Grace."

The older woman was indignant. "Of course I do. You've got to remember that I know D.B. I worked with him for years and I know how headstrong he can be. I knew if he got the letter he'd be forewarned and forearmed to send you on your way. As it is, you managed to catch him off guard."

Oh, Margo had certainly caught him off guard. And he definitely hadn't welcomed her. Just thinking about the things he'd said to her last night in the kitchen, the way he'd touched her, kissed her, still had the power to make her face burn. "I might have managed to stay here on the ranch for one night, but D.B. isn't a man to be shaken, Grace. I'm not getting anywhere with him."

"The will—"

"He hasn't given me an opportunity to discuss the will or anything else with him," Margo nearly shouted. "George wasn't thinking clearly when he sent me up here. This whole thing is nothing but a wild-goose chase!"

"Is this my cool, collected Margo talking? I've never heard you rattled like this before."

"D. B. Barlow is enough to rattle anybody's composure. The man is nothing but a cocky, obnoxious bas—" She stopped and sucked in a calming breath. "I'm just sorry I ever agreed to come up here."

"Don't talk that way, dear," Grace admonished her. "George is counting on you. He says if anyone can make his son listen to reason, it's you."

Margo pinched the bridge of her nose and blinked back the unexpected tears that had formed in her eyes. She couldn't remember the last time she'd felt the urge to cry. She couldn't remember the last time she'd allowed herself to cry. But with George being so ill, she desperately wanted to help him. He often called her the daughter he'd always hoped to have. How could she give up, knowing he put so much stock in her?

"George shouldn't put me on a pedestal," she said, her voice going quiet. "I'm only human. And since D. B. Barlow isn't, you might as well tell George that seeing his son back in Santa Monica looks about as remote as seeing snow there."

"I don't know what D.B. has said to you," Grace countered. "But I can tell you that he has a good, kind heart. He just doesn't want anyone to know it."

Margo grimaced. "I'd have to see an autopsy report on the man before I'd believe he possessed a heart," she told Grace. She then quickly added, "I've got to go. If you don't hear from me soon, you'll know I was probably killed by a bucking bronc, or I choked to death on all this clean air."

Grace laughed. "So you're a city girl. That doesn't mean you lack grit. You can do anything when you put your mind to it."

"That's stubbornness, Grace. Not grit."

"Well, honey, you'll need a lot of that, too, when you butt heads with D.B."

Margo agreed, but refrained from telling Grace exactly how she and D.B. had already butted more than heads. Instead she gave the woman a hasty goodbye and left the house. She knew if she didn't get down to the corrals soon, D.B. would think she'd backed out of their deal. And she'd never let him win that easily!

By the time Margo reached the stables, the holding pens connected to one side of them were already full of guests and saddled horses. Margo carefully climbed up on the fence and scanned the group for a glimpse of D.B.

"Say, Margo, are you gonna ride this morning?"

Margo turned her head to see the twins, Weston and Willis, riding up to her on a pair of chestnut ponies. Both boys had tied bright yellow kerchiefs around their necks and donned black cowboy hats with brims big enough to shade two faces. Apparently these boys were enthusiastic about their stay here. Too bad she couldn't say the same for herself.

"Yes, I will be riding, I think. Have you guys seen D.B. anywhere?"

"He's inside the horse barn," they answered in unison.

"Thank you," she told them. "Maybe we'll catch up to each other on the trail."

"That'd be great, Miss Margo," Weston said in a practiced drawl.

Willis scowled at his brother. "What are you calling her Miss Margo for? It's Ms., not Miss."

"That's not the cowboy way," Weston explained. "Don't you know how Gary Cooper done it? And in *Lonesome Dove,* Gus always said *Miss* Lorrie."

Willis let out a howl of laughter, but Margo didn't wait around to hear the rest of the argument. She left her perch on the fence and headed toward the stables. On the way she gave several horses a wide, wary berth. Were they all so tall and big?

Even though Margo's job kept her indoors most of the time, she wasn't averse to being out in the open air. As far as that went, she loved to go to the beach, walk in the sand and play in the surf. She enjoyed bicycling and riding behind someone on a motorcycle. But asking her to get on a horse was stretching things!

When she walked into the long barn, a mixture of smells assaulted her. There was the pungent scent of alfalfa hay mixed in with that of horses and sawdust and leather. Margo had never been in a barn. She'd never even been close to one before and as she looked around her she wondered what had made D.B. choose this life over the one he'd had in California.

She immediately spotted D.B. at the end of the building. He was silhouetted against an open doorway and the bright sunshine. As she walked toward him, down the long alleyway covered with sawdust, she noticed he was wearing a black Stetson with the brim pulled low over his forehead. Spurs were on his boots and the pale blue shirt he'd been wearing at breakfast had been replaced by a heavy blue denim with pearl snaps.

He was brushing a tall sorrel horse with four stockinged legs and seemed so intent on the job that she didn't think he realized she was anywhere near. It startled her when he spoke.

"I figured you'd backed out. I thought all I was going to see of you was the dust of your Jeep leaving."

"Then you figured wrong," she told him.

He tossed the brush over against the wall of the barn, then turned around to her. There was a challenging gleam in his eye and the sight of it made Margo's heart jerk against her breast.

"I guess I did," he said.

His voice was warm, the grin on his lips almost friendly. Margo could only stare at him and wonder what sort of game he was playing.

"Is this my horse?" she asked after a moment.

"It is," he told her. "His name is Ringo."

"As in Ringo Starr?" she asked, thinking a horse that was named after one of the Beatles couldn't be all bad.

Chuckling, D.B. reached for a saddle blanket that was lying over the top of a wooden railing. "No. I rather think this horse was named after the infamous outlaw Johnny Ringo."

Margo watched D.B. carefully smooth the nubby-textured blanket over the horse's back. Each movement of his hands was done slowly and deliberately, as though the task was as pleasing to him as stroking a woman's soft cheek. What would it be like, she wondered, if he were to touch her that way?

"Uh, I hope Ringo doesn't behave like an outlaw," she mused aloud.

D.B. tossed a thicker pad on top of the blanket, then glanced over his shoulder at Margo. She looked almost frightened and he felt something inside him melt like a gooey marshmallow.

"I don't have a mean animal on this place," he assured her, then motioned with his head for her to come closer. "Come here and I'll introduce you."

When she hesitated, he reached for her arm and yanked her over to him and the horse.

"Ringo won't hurt you," he said softly. "Believe me."

"I'm not so sure about that," she said in a breathy voice. "After all, you are trying to get rid of me."

"Not quite that literally," he said, then gently pulled the horse's head around to her. "Margo, this is Ringo. Give him a pat."

Margo looked up at the horse and then at D.B. "Will he bite?"

"No more than I do," he said, then laughed at her skeptical expression. "But he might take a little nibble," he added, his grin devilish.

Being this close to the horse unnerved her, but not nearly as much as having D.B. touching her, smiling at her as if she were just a woman. Not his father's lawyer. "It's been a long time since I've ridden. I—"

His features suddenly turned stony. "You told me you could do this. Or do you want to forget this whole thing and head on back to California this morning?"

His question instantly stiffened Margo's spine. Of course she didn't want to go back. Not without putting up her best fight first! "I have every intention of riding with you this morning."

"Good." He took her hand in his and gently placed it on the horse's glossy neck. "See. Ringo is a perfect gentleman. In fact, he's taken up with you already."

The horse sniffed at her hair, then gently nuzzled the side of her face with his nose. Smiling at the horse's display of affection, she looked up at D.B., who seemed content to keep her hand pressed beneath his. "I think he likes me," she said.

"I knew he would."

Then why don't you? D.B. could read the question in her eyes and it made him uncomfortable. Because he knew a part of him did like her and the other part was trying like hell not to.

He released her hand. Margo let out a long breath and glanced away from him. "I feel as if I should apologize to you," she said.

"Hmm. And why is that? You've decided I have blood in my veins instead of ice water?"

After being held next to his body, she could never doubt his being hot-blooded. "Oh, I'm sure you have blood in your veins, I'm just not sure what pumps it."

Laughing quietly, he reached for the saddle lying on a nearby hay bale. "I'll bet if you stuck your tongue out, it would look like a double-edged razor."

She purposely kept her tongue in her mouth and watched him effortlessly lift the saddle onto Ringo's back. She didn't know anything about horses or saddling them, yet she instinctively knew that D.B. was very much at home here in this horse barn. And that perplexed her. Where had this part of his life come from? Certainly not from George, who never set foot outside unless it was to get to his Mercedes.

"My tongue is perfectly normal," she informed him. "Though I'm not sure I can say the same for Grace."

He cocked his head around at her. "You jumped all over me last night about Grace. Now *you're* saying she isn't normal? This is a turnaround."

"Well, it's why I should apologize. I found out this morning that Grace never mailed that letter to you. The one telling you I was coming to the ranch. I'm sorry about that. I never dreamed she'd do such a thing."

He pulled on the cinch strap, tested the tightness, then buckled it down. "Grace has been in love with my father for years. She'd do anything for him." And apparently so would you, he thought.

Irritated by that idea, he snatched up Ringo's reins and quickly headed out the door, leaving Margo no choice but to hurry after him.

Out in the bright sunlight, D.B. led the horse a few steps around the corral, then indicated for Margo to get on him.

"Now?" she asked, unaware that she'd gasped the question.

He looked at her with dry impatience. "Yes, now. Unless you intend to walk. And I don't think you'd be able to keep up on foot."

Margo watched as his brown eyes fell to her boots. From the expression on his face, he didn't seem to consider them much better footwear than the high heels she'd been wearing last night.

Glancing around the corral, Margo saw that all the guests and a couple of wranglers were mounted and waiting for the two of them. With a sinking feeling in the pit of her stomach, she realized it was past the time for stalling.

Her mouth suddenly dry, she swallowed then said, "I'm ready."

D.B. tossed the reins over Ringo's neck. "Put your left hand on the saddle horn and your left foot in my hand. I'll give you a leg up," he instructed her.

She did as he said and the next instant Margo felt D.B.'s strength easily lift her up and into the saddle. Immediately she reached for the reins and stabbed her feet in the general direction of the stirrups. The movement of her heels against Ringo's sides instantly put the horse in a walk. Margo clutched the saddle horn and stared down at the ground, which appeared to be a neck-breaking distance away.

"Stop a minute," D.B. called to her. "Your stirrups need to be adjusted."

Margo looked helplessly at him and then the horse, who continued to lumber around the empty corral.

"Damn it, pull back the reins and say 'Whoa'!" D.B. yelled. "I thought you knew how to ride."

"I—I do. I did." Nervously she followed D.B.'s instructions and was relieved to see the horse stop at her command.

D.B. came over to her and Ringo and quickly reached for the leather strap beneath the fender of the saddle. With a quick jerk the stirrup lifted to the height of her dangling boot. "There's lots of horses in California," he said. "But it's obvious that none of them belong to you."

"No. But I do ride things," she said, feeling the need to defend herself. "I ride a bicycle, motorcycles and a surfboard."

"None of those things has a brain. Ringo does. So be careful with him and maybe he'll come through this unharmed."

Margo's mouth sagged open as he ducked under Ringo's head and went to work on the opposite stirrup.

"You're worried about the horse! What about me?" she asked incredulously.

He gave the piece of leather in his hands an equally hard jerk before glancing up at Margo. "You're supposed to be smarter than he is. So let's see if you are."

The goading grin on his face and the challenge in his eyes made Margo forget all about being afraid of Ringo. Her chin lifted airily as she met his gaze head-on.

"Lead the way, D.B. I'll be right behind you."

* * *

I'll be right behind you. Her promise turned out to be far easier said than done. The trail the group was taking led into the mountains and at times rimmed the edge with no more than a three- or four-foot passageway.

Margo had never seen such treacherous or beautiful country in her life. One minute her heart would be in her throat, wondering what little thing it might take to make Ringo toss her over the ledge of the mountain and into the green valley below. Then the next minute they would round yet another curve on the trail and Margo would marvel at the sheer beauty of the aspens and spruce, the rock bluffs and tall waterfalls.

"Getting tired, Margo?"

She looked up ahead of her to see D.B. had twisted around in his saddle to watch her. He was riding a spotted horse, the kind the Native Americans always rode in Western movies. Its sorrel-and-white coat glistened in the bright sunshine and its tail came close to dragging the ground. It was a magnificent, well-cared-for animal and very fitting for D.B., Margo decided. Paints were obviously a breed onto themselves. Just like him.

"I'm fine," she assured him. She'd die before she'd tell him that her back and legs were killing her, or that her hind end had gone numb with pain a mile back.

"Just wondering if you needed to turn back," he said.

Margo knew the innocent look of concern on his face was nothing but a put-on. It made her wonder if he ever felt anything for anyone. "No. There's no need to worry about me. Or Ringo. We're getting along fine." To further enforce her words, she patted the horse beneath her.

D.B. didn't say anything but inwardly he was smiling and shaking his head. By the time they returned to the ranch and Margo slid out of the saddle, she wouldn't be in any shape to argue his father's case. Whatever that might be.

"Miss Margo, see that old mine shaft up on the mountain? I'd like to climb up there and look for gold. Wouldn't you?"

"That looks like it might be dangerous," she said to Weston, who was riding directly behind her. The mine he'd pointed out was nothing more than a small cavity in the side of the mountain with a mound of yellow dirt directly below it. At one time a wooden awning had covered the entrance, but the boards had long ago rotted and fallen to one side.

"Ms. Kelsey is right," D.B. quickly spoke up. "It would be very dangerous. Those things could cave in at any given moment. Besides that, they're usually full of bats."

"Bats!" Weston and Margo exclaimed at the same time.

"Gee, wouldn't that be great." Willis spoke up as he rode closely behind his twin. "A brother who turns into a vampire."

Willis's remark set off an instant sparring of words between the two boys. Ignoring them, Margo continued to look at the old mine, which was located at least two thirds of the way up the mountain. It was incredible to her that anyone had ever reached the spot, much less worked there.

"Was there really ever gold up there?" she asked D.B.

"Why? Thinking of changing professions?"

She glared at him. How could she have kissed this man—and enjoyed it?

"Not hardly. I like the job I have."

Working for his father. Well, as far as D.B. was concerned, he'd rather face a cave full of bats than to have George Barlow interfering in every breath he took.

"No. I doubt there was ever gold in that mine," he told Margo. "These mountains are known for their veins of silver. But silver has little monetary value these days. It would cost more to mine it than what the mineral would be worth."

Margo gave the mine one last look. She'd never really been a history buff. At least not recent history. But as she looked at the old mine and the wild, rugged land around her, she could only imagine what it must have been like for those men who'd tried to prospect these mountains. They had either been very brave or very foolish to take on such a task and she told D.B. as much.

"A man has to have a vision, Margo. Or he's not much of a man."

For the first time, Margo agreed with D.B. Without a vision, a man or woman was lost in life. She could only wonder what his was.

"Is this your vision?" she asked him. "Running this dude ranch for the rest of your life?"

"It isn't just a dude ranch," he corrected her. "It's a real working ranch where cattle and horses are raised. And maybe that is my vision—to keep running this ranch. Even though you and my father think it's to go broke and embarrass him."

He turned back around in his saddle, taking away the opportunity for Margo to say more to him. For long moments she studied his broad shoulders and the smooth, easy way he sat his saddle. She hadn't known this was a real ranch. George hadn't told her that. And she was beginning to get the sneaking suspicion there was a lot more about D.B. that the older man hadn't told her.

They rode for another hour before D.B. called for a rest period. By then Margo could barely make it off Ringo. When her feet hit the ground, her legs felt as if they'd turned into two rubber bands.

Hoping no one was watching, she walked gingerly to a flat boulder and eased down into a sitting position. She didn't know how far these trail rides normally went, but this one had already lasted well into the afternoon. How much farther was the man going? she wondered. Was he trying to put her into so much misery, she'd be unable to walk, much less talk?

The question only made her more determined than ever to make it back to the ranch with the rest of the group, who seemed to be faring the trip in far better shape than herself.

Groaning, she closed her eyes and attempted to straighten her legs out in front of her.

"Gee, Miss Margo, you look awful!"

Margo opened her eyes to see that she'd been sandwiched in by the twins, who'd taken seats on the boulder with her. At the moment they were both staring at her with exaggerated concern.

"You must not be used to horseback riding." Willis spoke the obvious.

"Actually, I'm not," she told them, unable to conceal her weariness.

"You just wanted to try your hand at it, huh?" Weston asked.

"Something like that." Pushing at the loosened hair around her face, she scanned the group for a sight of D.B. She expected him to swoop down on her any minute and make some crude remark about her riding skills, or the lack of them.

"I guess you didn't know the Silver Spur is for veterans?"

Margo looked at the teenager. "Veterans?"

"Yeah," he answered. "You know, people who already know how to ride and are familiar with ranch life."

Great, she thought. She was the greenhorn around here. "I'm afraid that leaves me out."

"Don't worry, Miss Margo. Willis and I will take care of you. We'll show you the ropes."

"Thank you, guys. You're both real gentlemen." She only wished she could say the same for D.B. The only rope he'd probably be willing to show her was a hangman's noose.

For the next fifteen minutes most of the guests explored the bench of the mountain where they'd stopped to rest. Margo, who was too tired to breathe, stayed where she was until D.B. gave the word that it was time to mount up again.

Margo pushed herself to her feet and hobbled over to where Ringo was tied to the branch of a spruce tree.

"Are you going to be able to make it back to the ranch?"

It was D.B.'s voice and it was right at the back of her neck. Her pulse racing, she turned her head just enough to look at him from the corner of her eye. "I hardly have a choice, do I?"

He smiled at her, slowly, temptingly. "That depends. If you want to forgo our little talk, you can stay here and I'll come get you with the four-wheeler."

Ignoring the pain in her hind end, she did her best to smile back at him. "I wouldn't think of putting you to all that trouble."

A grin still on his lips, he reached out and lifted a strand of hair away from her cheek. "I'd understand if you didn't want to get back on Ringo," he said.

As the rough texture of his fingers brushed against her face, Margo forgot all about her pain.

"I'll just bet you'd understand," she murmured, hating the way her heart continued to jerk and pound just because this man had touched her. "But Ringo wouldn't. And since we've become friends on this ride, I don't want to disappoint him."

D.B. knew she was in pain, but he could also see that she was determined to see this challenge through. For one brief moment he felt badly about asking her on this trail ride. He hadn't really set out to hurt her. Quite frankly, he'd thought she would change her mind and turn back before she ever left the ranch.

But she hadn't turned back. She'd ridden for more than two hours, drooping wearily in the saddle and rubbing her legs when she thought he wasn't looking. What was driving this woman? Sheer grit, or the money she was bound to get from his father?

The question instantly washed away any guilt he'd been feeling and made his voice gruff when he spoke.

"Suit yourself."

"I'll make it," she said, more to assure herself than to make him a promise. "But since you're being so understanding, there is something you could do for me."

Turning to face him, she quickly slid out of her leather jacket. D.B.'s brows inched upward as his gaze slid over the thrust of her breast beneath the blue blouse she was wearing.

"This thing is too hot," she told him. "Would you tie it on my saddle?"

How could D.B. refuse when the sight of her without it was enough to make his mouth water?

He took the jacket and while rolling it up noticed the label inside the neck. The name was associated with an expensive shop on Rodeo Drive. Roxanne, his ex-fiancée, had shopped there. As long as she'd had the money, he grimly recalled.

"Aren't you afraid you'll mark it?" he asked, as he tied the jacket onto the skirt of the saddle.

Margo was too tired to notice the sarcasm in his voice. All she was worried about was making it back to the ranch without her body breaking into pieces.

Wiping her forearm across her brow, she said, "I'm not worried about a little jacket. My world doesn't revolve around clothes."

So just what did her world revolve around? D.B. wondered a few minutes later as the group of riders headed back to the Silver Spur. He had to admit as he watched her clinging wearily to the saddle horn and doing her best to stay upright, that he admired her.

She was turning out to be nothing like he'd first expected, and he was, in spite of all the warnings he'd given himself, becoming more and more intrigued with her.

Chapter Four

By the time the group of riders arrived back at the ranch, fingers of late-afternoon shadows were creeping across the cabins and corrals.

Margo was in such a state of exhaustion, everyone else had already turned their horses over to the stable hands when she was still trying to muster the strength to dismount.

"Need some help?"

She looked down to see D.B.'s arms stretched up to her. Too tired to question the gesture of kindness, she nodded, then reached for D.B.'s shoulders. At the same moment Ringo suddenly decided it was time for him to take a step forward.

Margo was instantly thrown off kilter and before she could catch hold of anything, she pitched sideways and straight into D.B.'s arms. He stumbled awkwardly backward but somehow managed to keep them both from falling to the ground as he took the brunt of her fallen weight against his chest.

"You nearly hit the dirt, city girl," he said, once he'd gotten a steadying grip on her waist.

The rough caress of his voice instantly righted Margo's senses, making her aware that she was clinging to him like a long-lost lover.

Her face aflame, she leapt away from him and didn't stop until there was a good five yards between them. "I—uh, sorry about that. I wasn't trying to knock you over."

"I didn't think you were."

Finding it impossible to meet his gaze, she worked at straightening her twisted clothing. "Uh, thank you for breaking my fall."

"I'm getting used to it," he said, his voice full of amusement. "In fact, if you stay around here much longer I'll get catching you down to perfection."

Her face grew even redder, if that was possible. No doubt he was thinking she was the weakest, most helpless woman he'd ever met!

"Hopefully for both of us, you won't be put to the test," she murmured.

Her embarrassment both surprised and touched D.B. From the moment she'd first set foot on the ranch, she'd made herself out to be a tough-hided businesswoman. But he was quickly beginning to see there was nothing tough about Margo Kelsey. "So. You made the ride and you kept up—are you ready for that talk now?"

Margo's head jerked up and she stared at him. Talk to him? She was so tired, she could barely function, must less have a serious discussion.

"Now? I need to clean up first."

D.B. shook his head. "I don't have time to wait. The ranch is giving a dance for the guests in the bunkhouse after supper. There's a lot I need to do."

"But you made a deal!" she came close to yelling.

He shrugged and studied her through lazy brown eyes. "I did. And since I am a man of my word you can talk to me later—at the dance. That is, if you're not too tired to attend."

A giant groan lodged in Margo's throat. A dance! How could she dance, when she wasn't even sure she could walk?

"Oh, I'll be there," she assured him, then drawing herself up as best she could, she turned and began the long walk back to the ranch house.

Thirty minutes later, Margo lay soaking in a tub of hot water and scented bath oil, thinking that no sane woman would have put herself through such a torturous ride. Every muscle in her body felt as if it had been stretched to the breaking point. Her back, her thighs, her calves were throbbing with pain, not to mention that unmentionable part that felt as if she'd been straddling a fence for twenty-four hours.

Oh, dear George, she groaned inwardly. He'd given her so much. An important position at Barlow and Associates and a hefty salary that assured her financial security. But those two things were not the reasons Margo was willing to go to such lengths to help the older man. Over the past three years she'd grown to love George Barlow. He'd welcomed her into his home and treated her like a daughter. And for Margo, who could only remember a succession of deadbeat stepfathers passing in and out of her young life, George had become the father she'd always yearned for. He was there for her when she needed someone to count on. Suffering through a horseback ride was the least she could do for the man.

Margo soaked for thirty more minutes, then decided she'd better get out if she was going to make it to the dance.

Wrapping a towel around her, she walked back through to the bedroom and immediately spied her leather jacket lying across the bed.

It hadn't been there before. Come to think of it, she'd forgotten and left the garment tied to Ringo's saddle. Apparently D.B. had brought it in while she'd been soaking in the tub and placed it right beside the lace bra and panties she'd laid out.

A flush spread across her face at the idea of D.B. looking at her intimate apparel, even though she told herself it was nothing to be embarrassed about. She was a grown woman and D.B. was a mature man. No doubt he'd seen plenty of women in and out of their underwear.

Well, Margo thought ruefully, at least he could only guess as to what she looked like in pink lace bikinis.

Another hour passed before she finished dressing in a light blue peasant dress and walked down to the bunkhouse. When she entered the big building it was to see that the long tables and benches had been removed from the center of the room and a crowd of people were already dancing to recorded music.

Across the room against one wall, two long tables had been set up with food and drinks. Margo hadn't eaten since she'd returned from the ride, so she carefully made her way through the crowd and began to fill a paper plate with an assortment of finger foods.

"We thought you weren't coming."

Margo glanced up at the twins who were still wearing their hats, but had changed into matching plaid shirts. She smiled at both of them. "It took me a little longer than usual to get ready," she explained. "Has the party been going on long?"

Weston nodded. "Me and Willis have already danced with every woman here."

There were ten women among the group of guests, all of which Margo had learned were here with their husbands. Margo was the only single woman on the ranch. Besides making her feel conspicuous, it made her wonder if single women ever came to this place. Surely D.B. didn't live a celibate life up here. A man like him couldn't live that way, could he?

Determined to push the question out of her thoughts, she turned her attention back to the twins. "Then you guys must already be danced out," she remarked.

"Oh, no, we've been waiting for you," Willis quickly informed her. "Can you do the two-step?"

Normally Margo could follow most any dance step, but tonight she was doing well just to walk. Still, she wasn't about to sit like a wallflower all evening and give D.B. the impression he'd very nearly crippled her. "I can try. Later, after I've eaten," she promised the teenagers.

For those who wanted to sit and eat or take a break from the dancing, benches rimmed the walls of the large room. Margo carried her plate over to an empty spot while Weston and Willis promptly fetched her a cup of coffee, a napkin and silverware.

As she ate and listened to the boys chatter on about their school and their parents back in Kansas, Margo discreetly watched D.B. mill about the crowd.

He was dressed simply in blue jeans, white shirt and black cowboy boots. Tonight he was hatless and his dark hair waved with abandon about his face. He seemed completely at home and totally relaxed among the crowd, as though he considered them friends and family instead of paying guests. And maybe he truly did think of them in that way, she thought. One thing was for sure, there was a completely different side to D.B. than the arrogant cynical man he showed Margo.

She was dancing with Willis, for the third time, when D.B. tapped the teenager on the shoulder. "Mind if I take over?"

Willis graciously handed Margo over to D.B. "She dances real good, Mr. Barlow. A lot better than she rides."

"I'm glad to hear that, Willis," D.B. said with a laugh, then pulled Margo into his arms.

"I don't know whether to feel insulted or flattered," Margo said, as D.B. began to move her to the slow country tune that was playing.

D.B. grinned down at her. "Believe me, those boys think you're the best thing to come along since sliced bread."

Margo had done her share of dancing through the years, but it had never felt like this, she realized. D.B.'s hand was wrapped around hers, while his arm curved tightly against her back. Her face was only a scant inch or two from his chest and each time she glanced up, his dented chin and roughly hewn lips were there to taunt her.

"And I suppose you excuse them for liking me because they're young and impressionable boys," she said after a moment.

"They don't need an excuse. You're a beautiful woman."

Taken by complete surprise, she glanced up at him. "Are you trying to flatter me into leaving?"

One of his dark brows arched inquisitively. "Flatter you? Not hardly. A woman smart enough to be the legal adviser for a multimillion dollar business should be smart enough to see through a man's flattery. No, I was just stating a fact. One that I'm sure you're aware of."

The dash of warmth she'd felt at his compliment suddenly vanished. "Contrary to what you might think, I don't usually have men gathered around me, telling me how beautiful I am."

There was such a prim, frosty look on her face that D.B. just had to laugh. "You don't? Well, what about one man hanging around you, telling you that you're beautiful?"

Margo's personal life was really none of his business, but she could hardly tell him that. Not when she'd been trying to get personal information from him since the moment she'd arrived on the ranch.

"No. Not even one man."

The arm against her back began to slide upward until his fingers were at the edge of her low-backed dress. Margo did her best not to shiver as the rough texture of his hand moved against her soft skin.

"And why is that?" he asked lowly. "You don't have time for men? Or you just don't like them?"

As he waited for her answer, he studied her face, the smoothness of her skin, the soft delicate lines of her lips and nose, the gently rounded chin that had thrust itself at him more than once. He couldn't imagine this woman without a man in her life, a man who would appreciate her beauty, fill her blue eyes with passion.

She shrugged but it did nothing to loosen his hold on her. "I like men," she assured him. "I just don't depend on them to make me happy."

"What an odd thing to say."

Margo could see from the look on his face that she'd bewildered him. "It's not really odd," she explained. "It's just that down through the years I've learned that most men are users. They make a lot of promises, but in the end they only take."

The music came to an end just as D.B. was wondering if she'd already grouped him with the majority. Margo waited expectantly for him to release her. When he didn't, she looked up at him.

"You can go another round or two, can't you?" he asked.

He was smiling at her, and from the glint in his eyes, Margo could see he was either testing her or teasing her. Either way, she found it impossible to pull away from him.

"Of course I can. Why couldn't I?"

D.B. knew that each step she took was probably killing her. Still, she was putting on a brave face. When he'd first met her last night, he hadn't expected that today he would be admiring her for grit and tenacity. But he couldn't help being impressed by the physical endurance she'd shown him today. "Oh, I just thought you might be a little . . . sore."

The music started up again and D.B. began to move her into a slow two-step that was really nothing more than an unconscious shuffle. Margo felt like wailing. Each move she made sent shafts of pain through her body, and every moment she was in his arms like this was proving to be sheer torture for her senses.

"Why, no. What makes you think I'm sore? I visit the gym on a regular basis and my trainer says I'm in good shape."

Oh, there was definitely nothing wrong with her shape, D.B. thought. Every inch of her was soft and inviting. And having her here in his arms like this was a temptation he was finding very hard to resist. In fact, he didn't want to resist it. He wanted this dance with her to keep going and going.

Disgusted with himself, he drew in a long breath and with it the scent of crushed roses. The sweet perfume on her skin plus the feel of her warm body against his were playing powerfully on his senses. D.B. knew, for his own sake, he had to get on with business.

"So, now that you're here and I'm here, are you ready to talk?"

Margo glanced nervously up at him. "You mean about your father?"

D.B. grimaced. The last thing he wanted to do was talk about his father, but he didn't see any way around it. Not without a fight from her. "I mean about whatever it is you came here to talk about. If it's about my father, then so be it. I promised you that much and—"

"And you're a man who keeps his promises," she finished for him, then tilted her head back so that she could look him straight in the face.

"Always," he murmured, his eyes drawn to the soft, full line of her lips.

His arm tightened against her back, causing her breast to press against him. Margo suddenly wondered if he could feel the throb of her heart and if he knew that he was the sole reason for its erratic behavior.

"Then, yes, I am ready to talk. But I'd really rather it be somewhere a little quieter than this," she told him, knowing there was no way she could form one sensible sentence as long as she remained in his arms.

"I can remedy this," he told her and quickly led her off the dance floor.

Still holding on to her hand, he skirted the crowd, then led her through the kitchen.

"Where are we going?" she asked.

"Somewhere quiet. That is what you wanted?"

Margo knew she could hardly argue with him now, so she merely nodded and allowed him to tug her out a back door and into the cool night.

As they walked away from the bunkhouse, D.B. said, "Look at that sky, Margo. Did you ever see one like that back in L.A.?"

Margo lifted her head and for several moments studied the clear night sky. It blazed with thousands of stars, some of them so vivid, she felt she could almost reach up and touch them.

"No, I'm afraid we're not blessed with this clean of air." She pulled her eyes down from the sky to look at him. "But then you knew that."

A wry expression touched his face. "Well, even though it's been awhile since I was there, I was pretty sure L.A. hadn't lost its smog."

He let go of her hand, but continued to walk. Margo kept pace beside him while fiercely telling herself she really didn't miss the touch of his fingers on hers. She only missed the security his hold had given her as they walked over the dark, rocky ground.

Annoyed with herself, she folded her hands together and deliberately kept her eyes in front of her. "You sound as if you don't miss Los Angeles," she mused aloud.

He chuckled under his breath as though he found her remark ridiculous. "Would you?" he asked, then quickly shaking his head, he laughed again. "That's a stupid question. Of course you'd miss it. The bright lights, the luxuries, the conveniences, the entertainment and shopping. I can see where a woman like you would go crazy up here."

A woman like her? Just what kind of woman did he think she was? Frivolous? Shallow? "I might miss L.A., but I like to think I'm strong enough to adapt to any place—if I had to."

She might adapt, D.B. thought, but she damned sure wouldn't be happy.

Neither one of them said any more until they reached the stables. By then Margo was shivering as goose bumps danced across her skin. Whether she was reacting from the cold, or from being alone with D.B., she didn't know.

"You're going to freeze to death in that dress," D.B. said as the two of them entered the dimly lit barn.

Margo hugged her arms against her breast. She'd worn this dress several times before and never felt a bit self-conscious. So why did D.B.'s gaze make her feel as if she were half-naked? "When I put it on, I didn't know I was going to be outside," she explained. "Is it always this cold at night up here?"

"No. Most of the time it's a lot colder," he said. Then he added, "Wait here. I'll be right back."

He went through a door just to the left of her. When a light came on inside it, Margo could see it was a tack room filled with saddles, bridles and all sorts of horse gear.

Margo stood where she was and waited. After a moment D.B. reappeared through the door. A fleece-lined jacket was slung across his arm.

"Here," he said, draping the garment around her bare shoulders. "I don't want you catching cold."

The thoughtful gesture completely disarmed her, though she did her best to cover it with a little laugh. "Why? Afraid I'll be stuck here on the ranch a little longer?"

Funny, but the idea of her being here didn't bother D.B. nearly as much as it had last night. "No, I just wouldn't want you to take a bad impression of Colorado back with you."

He started down the alleyway and Margo followed. "The impression I leave here with will be entirely up to you, not the weather," she told him.

He stopped at one of the stalls and hooked his arms over the top of the gate. Twisting his head around to her, he gave her an impish smile. "How am I doing so far?" he asked.

The more Margo thought she was beginning to know this man, the more she realized she didn't. At times she got the real impression he was flirting with her. But she couldn't imagine why. He didn't like her. He'd already spelled that out quite clearly.

"It's too early to tell," she said as she came to a halt a step or two away from him.

His expression swiftly turned sober. "You know, Wanda had the idea that you might have come here to sue me. Is that what this is all about? The old man has finally figured out the ultimate way to degrade me?"

Margo's mouth fell open. "Sue you? Of course not! Your father loves you!"

D.B. threw back his head and laughed. "I thought lawyers were supposed to be able to read people, to know when they were being lied to."

"What's that supposed to mean?"

"It means, Margo, that my father has hoodwinked you. He doesn't love me. In fact, I'm not sure that he's ever loved anyone."

Amazed, she said, "You don't believe that. You couldn't."

"I think it's rather presumptuous of you to be telling me what I believe."

The words were softly spoken, yet they were edged with warning. Even so, Margo decided to move closer to him, to take a chance that he wouldn't shut her out completely.

"Maybe I am being presumptuous," she said quietly. "But I can't fathom your thinking. Where do you get the idea that George doesn't love you? From all accounts I've seen, he thinks the sun rises and sets in you."

D.B. let out a snort of disbelief. "Twenty years ago, hearing that would have meant something to me. I would have believed it, because I would have wanted to believe it. Back then I was willing to do anything to gain my father's love and approval. Now it means nothing."

Twenty years ago he would have been an impressionable teenager, Margo mentally calculated. "What happened?"

"What happened?" he echoed mockingly. "It's simple. I grew up. I realized that my father didn't want a son to love. He wanted someone to control and manipulate."

Another spasm of shivering hit her, making her draw the lapels of the jacket closer together. "All fathers are that way to a certain extent. Or at least I hear they are," she said in afterthought.

D.B. glanced at her, his expression clearly incredulous. "So this is what you came all the way up here to tell me? That my father says he loves me and that I should forgive him?"

Shaking her head, she leaned her hip against the wooden gate. "Well, not exactly. I'm here because..." She paused, drew in a shaky breath, then lifted her eyes to his stony face. "After your father had the heart attack, he had me draw up a new will. I'm here—"

D.B. threw up a hand before she could go any further. "There's no need for you to go on. I don't care what's in the will," he said sharply.

A part of Margo had feared D.B. would react this way. From the moment she'd met him, she could see that he was a man who lived by his own rules and values. And he didn't appear to value any of the things that his father did.

"But you might! George has—"

"Made you the beneficiary? Well, all I can say is more power to you."

Margo gasped. "Are you crazy?"

"Not since I left George and the corporate world behind," he pointed out with a great amount of sarcasm.

"Well, I'm not sure I'm convinced," she countered hotly.

Frustrated, he raked his fingers through his hair, then pushed himself away from the stall gate. "Look, Margo. Like I told you this morning, the last thing I want is for my father to be ill. I'm very sorry that he has been and I hope with everything inside me that he gets better, but I'm not interested in what George does with his money."

"It's not just the money, or the home in Beverly Hills," Margo hastened to inform him. "He's going to give the whole business to you. Barlow and Associates will be yours. All you have to do is go back to California and help your father run the investment firm. That's all he asks of you."

The shadows in the barn did little to hide the disgust on D.B.'s face. "Now why didn't I see that coming? I know better than anyone that George only gives to get something back." His steps halted and he turned to face her. "Tell me I'm wrong about that, too," he dared.

Margo couldn't understand why she suddenly felt a need to comfort this man. But as she looked up at his dark, brooding face, she knew with startling clarity that this man had a cold void inside him, an emptiness that comes with feeling unloved.

But how could she assure this man? How could she convince him that his father truly loved him?

"No. I won't tell you that you're wrong," she said softly. "Because I think that is exactly what George is doing. I think he'd give anything to get you back."

For long moments D.B. stared unseeingly at the black loft above their heads. "Margo, I'm sure you can't understand this, but I gave some of the best years of my life to Barlow and Associates. I don't intend to give them what I have left," he said firmly.

"But I don't think you really realize what you'd be giving up. The whole world has been in recession, yet your father's business continues to grow. Its worth is . . . staggering to say the least."

He glanced down at her and his lips twisted into a cynical smile. "I know the worth of Barlow and Associates. After all, I was the CPA there. And it doesn't surprise me that the business has continued to grow. Everything my father touches somehow manages to turn a monetary gain. I suppose it's because money is sacred to him. He knows money equals power. And power is everything to my father."

"You make him sound like a greedy, horrible man. And that simply isn't true. Since I've gone to work for your father, he's been nothing but generous."

"And how long have you worked for my father?" he asked curiously.

"Three years."

So she must have come to work shortly after he'd left Santa Monica, he concluded. At least that explained why he'd never seen her around the office building.

"And you like it?"

Why was he asking? she wondered. She didn't fit into any of this. She was merely acting as a messenger.

"Very much," she answered. "I'm in charge of the whole legal team at Barlow and I love the challenge. And since I know you're wondering...yes, George gives me a very generous salary."

From what D.B. could see, she was certainly doing her best to earn it. Or was she trying to do more than just earn her salary? Maybe there was some other motive that had pushed her into coming all the way up here to the Colorado mountains.

"Uh—you and my father—you've gotten close?"

Her eyes wide, Margo stared at him. "How close do you mean?" she asked, her voice suddenly frosty.

"I think you know what I mean."

"You're implying that—" Margo shook her head in complete disbelief. "George is old enough to be my father!"

"That's never stopped lesser men than him. Besides, my father is still a handsome man."

Turning, he moved on down the sawdust-covered alleyway. As Margo watched him walk away, she decided not to be insulted by his suggestion. After all, D.B. couldn't know what had been happening in his father's life for the past three years. And she realized the more they talked about his father, the more opportunity she would have of arguing her case to him.

Catching up with him, she said, "For what it's worth, I think your father is in love with Grace. And we both know she's crazy about him. It wouldn't surprise me if they married someday. Would that bother you?"

D.B. was relieved. For some foolish reason, he couldn't bear to think Margo might have been romantically involved with his father. Not that he expected George to live the life of a monk. He didn't care if he had ten girlfriends, or even a wife. He just knew that Margo needed someone closer to her own age. She needed a man who could raise her temperature a notch or two. A man like himself.

"Hell, no. It wouldn't bother me," he said. "In fact, he can leave Barlow and Associates to her. Although, I wouldn't wish it on my worst enemy."

"You really mean that, don't you?"

"Damn right, I mean it."

"I can't understand you," Margo said, completely bewildered by his attitude. "How could you turn something like this down—without even thinking about it?"

"Easy," he answered. "I didn't like my life there. This one is much better. I've found I love this simple life up here in the mountains. At least here my father isn't standing over my shoulder trying to tell me what to do, or how to do it. I can't go back to that.''

One of the horses hung his head over the stall door. D.B. stopped to stroke its black nose and ears. Margo stood a step away from him and quietly appreciated the gentle way he treated the horse.

"You know," she said, her voice unknowingly wistful, "when I was growing up, I would have given anything for a father. A father who loved me enough to stick around and teach me all the things I needed to know to survive in this world."

D.B.'s hand stilled against the horse's face. "You didn't have a father?"

"No. He died when I was too small to remember. From what my mother has told me, we were very poor at the time. She was uneducated and forced to work at anything she could find to support herself and a child." Margo heaved a heavy sigh as she remembered those unhappy days of her childhood. "Eventually Mother decided the answer to our needs was a man. A man could take care of us, give us a nice home where we could all be a family together. It never happened. But bless Mother's heart, she tried. I saw five different stepfathers come and go, and all that time we lived in nothing better than a run-down rented house, or a cheap apartment."

D.B. looked at her and the melancholy he saw on her face was so real, it stabbed him right in the heart. How had she survived? he wondered sickly. She hadn't even had a father—much less a home.

"I'm sorry, Margo. I can't imagine how that must have been for you."

Reaching out, she stroked the horse's long nose. "It could have been worse," she said, trying her best to put a cheery note in her voice. "Anyway, I didn't tell you this to gain your sympathy. I was trying to make a point."

Turning to her, D.B. gently framed her face with his hands. Margo stood stock-still, her heart beating wildly in her throat.

"And what is the point, Margo?"

She had the feeling that his mind wasn't really waiting on her answer. There was a hungry look in his eyes. A hunger that had nothing to do with food or money.

"That you should appreciate having a father who loves you. That money isn't something to be shunned simply because you're fortunate enough not to be poor."

He shook his head. "Margo, I can see why you'd tend to put more of a value on money than me. But take it from me, the stuff isn't a cure-all. It's not a source of happiness."

How could a man like him, a man who'd never had to want for anything, say that to her? She'd had to scratch and claw, do without and work long, bone-tiring hours to have the things she had now.

"You stand here and talk about peace of mind being the most important thing to you, but tell me, D.B., just how much peace of mind could you have if you had to worry where your next meal was coming from?"

His hands dropped from her face and took hold of her shoulders. Even through the jacket, Margo could feel the strength of his fingers dipping into her flesh.

"If you think your high-powered job and the money it gives you will always keep you happy, then I really feel sorry for you," he growled.

"And I feel sorry for you," she swiftly countered. "You have a wonderful father who loves you, who's trying to give you everything."

His face turned as hard as granite. "I don't need my father or his money to make me happy."

Without thinking, her hands came up and curled around his forearms. "You know, D.B.," she whispered, "I'm wondering if you really know what happiness is. I'm beginning to wonder if you're actually up here in the mountains to hide."

"Hide?" He sneered at the question.

"Yes, hiding away from the truth, because you're not man enough to face the problems you have with your father."

Anger rose up in D.B. like a giant tidal wave, making the hold he had on Margo's shoulders tighten to a grip. "Since you want to constantly question my manhood," he gritted fiercely, "maybe I should prove myself with actions instead of words."

"That isn't—"

Before she could get another word past her lips, D.B. jerked her into his arms. She landed against his massive chest, her face buried in the folds of his shirt. The warmth and scent of his body instantly overwhelmed her and in a panic she tried to push away from him.

The movement caused the jacket to slip from Margo's shoulders. Cool air wafted over her bare skin, then suddenly his hands were on her upper arms sending shock waves of heat reverberating through her body.

Stunned by the intensity of his touch, Margo sagged against him. To D.B., her soft skin was like an invitation to heaven and his fingers glided over her smooth shoulders, up the sides of her neck and finally to her face.

With his thumb beneath her chin, he tilted her face back and looked into her eyes. "You want me to kiss you, don't you?"

How could he ask her? And how could he be so right? she wondered wildly. "No," she whispered.

The corners of his mouth curved upward into a knowing smile. "Then why don't you move away from me?"

Chapter Five

Margo swallowed as a strange yearning began to build inside her. "I can't. You—you're holding me," she answered.

"That's right," D.B. pointed out, his voice dropping to a husky murmur. "But I'm not holding you that tightly."

He was right. She could move out of his embrace if she wanted to. But the shocking truth was, Margo didn't want to move. She wanted to feel his hands on her face, wanted the warmth and hardness of his body next to hers.

"You're crazy!" she breathed.

The smile on his face deepened, giving Margo a glimpse of his white teeth. "You're right. Holding you like this proves it. But I'm also a *man*. Something you seem to frequently forget."

Margo opened her mouth to defend herself, but before she could utter one word, D.B.'s face drew downward. By the time his lips had fastened over hers, Margo was past pretending. Crazy or not, she wanted this man to kiss her. And she didn't care if he knew it.

Beneath his, her lips parted, sending him an invitation to deepen the kiss. D.B. didn't need further encouragement. The taste of her lips was like pure honey, almost overpowering in its sweetness. The more he tasted, the more he wanted.

Before Margo realized what was happening to her, she was responding fervently to the heated search of his lips. Groaning low in her throat, her arms lifted and curled around his neck, her small body arched into him.

Desire, swift and all consuming, swept through D.B., blinding him to where they were and why. He wanted nothing more than to pull away the ice-blue dress she was wearing, lay her down in the hay and worship every inch of her body. He wanted to feel the warmth of her body give in to his. And maybe then he wouldn't feel the awful ache inside him, the emptiness that had followed him from California.

Margo was so lost in the little kisses he was planting along her neck, she hardly noticed when he began to slowly move her backward. And even when he lowered her down on a stack of hay, she didn't question him. Rather, she clung to him, unwilling to break the cloud of magic that swirled around them.

D.B. had only planned to kiss her. Once. But that one kiss had set off a fire storm inside him. Now he couldn't get Margo close enough to quench the flames.

The hay was rough and scratchy against Margo's back, but she was oblivious to the discomfort. While D.B.'s mouth hungrily searched hers, his hands seemed to be everywhere. They touched her face, her arms, her throat and finally the edge of her bodice where a gentle tug of his fingers caused the gathered fabric to slip over her shoulders and down to her waist.

"Margo, you're so beautiful, so soft," he whispered as his lips slid down her throat, then even lower to the valley between her breasts.

The sound of his voice was as intoxicating as his touch. By the time he pushed away the flimsy bra she was wearing, she was aching for his lips to find her breast. When they did, she gasped and dug her fingers deeper into the muscles of his back.

Knowing she was swiftly losing all control, Margo struggled to pull her drugged senses back together. "D.B., this is—"

Her whispered words hung unfinished as he lifted his head and looked down at her. "Good," he finished in a strained voice. "And it will be even better if you'll let me make love to you."

Make love. Yes! She wanted that more than anything. But this man didn't want to make love. He wanted sex. Nothing more. Nothing less.

"D.B., I—"

Before she could murmur another word, his hand slipped beneath her skirt to cradle the intimate part of her with his palm. To have him touching her in such a way was almost Margo's undoing. White-hot desire flashed through her, and for the first time in her life she wanted a man with every fiber of her being.

But she couldn't allow it to happen, she silently screamed. Not with a man who despised her!

"No. D.B., I can't!"

The instant her choked words were out, D.B. rolled away from her. Margo jerked her clothing back into place then bolted from the hay and ran blindly down the alleyway through the rows of horse stalls.

"Margo, wait!"

His call to her wasn't demanding. In fact, it was a plea that echoed the yearning inside Margo. But she didn't let it sway her into stopping. Nor did she look back at him as she ran out of the barn. She was afraid if she did, she'd run straight back to his arms.

Outside, the bunkhouse was still ablaze with lights and music. Margo hurried past it and on to the ranch house. By the time she reached the porch, she was completely out of breath and shaking uncontrollably. However, she didn't so much as pause until she was inside her bedroom with the door shut firmly behind her.

Dear God, what was happening to her?

Sinking down on the edge of the bed, Margo held her hand to her heaving chest. She wasn't just out of breath from her run, she was terrified. She'd come close, so achingly close to giving herself to D. B. Barlow. What had come over her?

Jumping to her feet, she crossed to the dresser and stared at herself in the mirror. Her face was flushed, her lips swollen. Bits of alfalfa clung to her hair and her dress was crushed with a mass of wrinkles. But her disheveled appearance was nothing compared to the ache of desire that was still throbbing through her body, begging her to go back to him.

Amazed by it all, Margo eased down on a vanity bench and slowly passed trembling hands over her face. Margo had dated, and she'd been in some intimate situations before. But never had she felt with those men, the things she'd just experienced in D.B.'s embrace. What did it mean?

Too afraid to answer that question, Margo grabbed the hairbrush and scraped it painfully against her scalp. Whatever it meant didn't matter. She wasn't going to let it happen again. In fact, she wasn't going to stay around to let it happen.

Tossing aside the hairbrush, she stripped away her dress, then wrapped herself in a bathrobe. Back at the bedside, she reached for the telephone on the nightstand.

Once the number was punched through, Margo nervously twined the coiled line between her fingers and waited for an answer.

"Barlow residence."

She instantly recognized the housekeeper's voice. "Sadie, this is Margo Kelsey. Has Mr. Barlow retired for the evening?"

"No, Ms. Kelsey. He's in his library. If you'll hold just a moment, I'll connect you."

Seconds later, George's voice came over the line and Margo unconsciously gripped the receiver. "George, it's Margo here. How are you?"

"Margo! It's so good to hear your voice. I've been thinking about you."

Margo swallowed the lump that had suddenly collected in her throat. "You sound tired, George. You haven't made yourself sick worrying about all this, have you?"

"No! I haven't had another heart attack, if that's what you're getting at. And I'm not worrying. Why should I, now that you're there on the ranch with D.B.?"

As if that could fix anything, Margo silently groaned. "Well, actually D.B. is the reason I'm calling—"

"He's coming home? He's agreed to the proposal of the will?"

The eager sound in the older man's voice tore at Margo's heart. But she had to be truthful with him. At least that would be easier than setting him up for a harder fall later on. "No. I'm afraid D.B. isn't interested in coming back to the firm, George. He says he's happy here."

The silence on the other end of the line continued for so long that Margo suddenly became worried. Had D.B.'s father collapsed? "George? George, are you still there?"

He bellowed out a curse. "Hell, yes, I'm here. I'm just thinking."

Margo let out a sigh of relief. "Thank goodness. You scared me."

George snorted. "Don't worry, Margo. I'm not about to die—at least not until my son comes home to me."

Shaking her head, Margo passed a weary hand through her tangled hair. "George, look, you need to know that D.B. is bitter. In my opinion I can't ever see him changing his mind about this."

"I know D.B. is bitter. He thinks I've tried to run his life. And maybe I did," George admitted with a tired sigh. "But I've learned my lesson. If he'll just come home, I won't smother him. I'll let him be who or what he wants to be."

Margo took a seat on the bed. "He wants to be a rancher."

"Hell, he's had that uncivilized notion in his head since he was a young kid. Why, I'll never understand! The boy is wasting his brain up there. Not to mention the rest of his life."

Margo wasn't going to argue with George. For one thing she knew it wasn't good for his health. And now that she was here on the ranch and beginning to know D.B., she was seeing things from a different perspective. "It's not so bad up here, George. He could do worse."

"Don't tell me you're starting to like it up there?" he asked incredulously.

"Well, the mountains are beautiful. And I rode a horse today," she added with a great amount of pride.

"A horse! My Lord, how did that happen?"

How had any of this happened? she asked herself. It seemed each time she got within a foot or two of D.B., everything happened. "Uh, your son suggested it. And he can be very persuasive, believe me."

George laughed. "That's my son. He's damn good-looking, too, isn't he?"

She smiled with sad resignation. "Yes. He takes after his father. But, George, I think the only thing for me to do now is come home. There's nothing else I can do here for you."

"Margo, you can't come home! Not yet! You just got there."

Maybe she had, but to Margo it felt like she'd been here for days. "George, do you realize how difficult this is for me? For heaven's sake, D.B. resents my being here. He doesn't want me around!"

To her amazement, George laughed. "A woman like you? My son might be a rancher now instead of a CPA, but I know he couldn't have changed his mind about beautiful women."

Annoyed with him, she said, "George, I'm not here to flirt, cajole or seduce your son! I've told him about the will. Now I'm coming home."

"Why are you being so defensive? I wasn't proposing anything of the sort. I merely want you to stay a little longer. Try to reason with him. Please."

Somewhat mollified, she said, "He's not interested in money and he seems to abhor the idea of working in the business world again."

"Does he have a woman up there with him?" George asked suddenly.

"A woman? No. Why... ?"

"Then you tell him about the rest of the will, Margo."

Margo suddenly felt ill. "George, I don't think—"

"I'm not asking you to think, just tell him."

"George, I just told you he doesn't have a woman," she shot back.

"Then he'd better find one—fast. I don't know how much longer this ticker of mine is going to last."

Margo reluctantly agreed, but after she'd told the older man good-night and hung up the telephone, she had to fight the urge to call him back. She didn't want to stay here on the Silver Spur. Especially now that D.B. knew just how attracted she was to him.

Attracted! What an understatement! She'd been on fire for the man. She'd almost made love to him! Now she had to find some legitimate reason for staying a few days longer. Dear God, how was she going to do it?

"Is your visitor still here?"

Wanda's question had D.B. glancing up from the coffee cup he'd been staring moodily into for the past five minutes. "Yes. But I expect she's probably up and packing by now."

Wanda turned away from her chopping board to cast her boss a sly look. "I guess you're glad she's leaving."

"Is that a question?" he asked, impatient with Wanda for bringing up the subject of Margo. He didn't want to think about her leaving. Because a part of him wasn't quite ready for her to go. Yet he didn't want to think of her staying, either. If she stayed, he didn't know how he was going to keep his hands off her.

"Well," Wanda said as she went back to dicing onions and jalapeño peppers, "yesterday you implied you couldn't get rid of her fast enough. But last night you were cozying up to her on the dance floor like—"

"I want you to go up to Gunnison and get your eyes checked, Wanda. Apparently you're not seeing right."

Chuckling more to herself than to him, Wanda tossed the vegetables into a bowl of raw eggs. "Ain't a thing wrong with my eyesight, D.B."

"There must be. Because I certainly wasn't cozying up to Margo," he growled in denial.

Undaunted by the scowl on D.B.'s face, Wanda gave him a knowing smile. "All I can say is if you'd danced with those other women the way you danced with Ms. Kelsey, you would've had a lot of mad husbands on your hands."

Snorting, D.B. got up from the table and dumped his coffee into the sink. When he went to the coffeemaker and began pouring himself another cup, Wanda said, "I guess you know what you're doing."

"My coffee was cold. I'm getting more. If you don't mind," he added tersely.

"Don't mind at all. But it wouldn't have gotten cold if you'd been drinking the stuff instead of staring at it."

"Why do I let you work here?" he asked with a wry shake of his head.

Cackling, Wanda poured the eggs into a skillet. "You *let* me, because I'm the best damn cook you could find who would stay back in these mountains eight or nine months out of a year. Besides that, you like me."

It was true; he did like Wanda. She might be nosy, but she would bend over backward to help him if he needed it.

Grinning at her, he said, "And you're damn lucky I do, too."

Just as Wanda started to make a retort, a knock sounded at the open doorway leading into the kitchen. Both D.B. and the cook turned to see Margo hovering on the threshold.

"I hope I'm not intruding," she said brightly, "but I wondered if I might beg a cup of coffee from you."

"Why sure, Ms. Kelsey," Wanda quickly told her. "Come on in and I'll pour you a cup. That is, if D.B. hasn't dumped it all down the drain."

D.B. arched a brow at the older woman. What in hell had gotten into Wanda, anyway? She never allowed guests back here in her kitchen, upsetting her routine and getting in the way. Now she was inviting Margo in like she was an old friend.

Margo stepped into the room and D.B. felt everything inside him react to her presence. She was wearing a pair of black jeans and a white cotton shirt. Several buttons were undone at the throat, tempting D.B.'s gaze to travel downward to the thrust of her breasts.

The sight of her soft curves reminded D.B. of just how perfect she'd felt in his arms, and the awful ache she'd left him with when she'd run from the barn.

"Good morning, D.B.," Margo said, bravely meeting his gaze as she took a seat at the small kitchen table.

The pit of his stomach quivered as he looked into her blue eyes. "Good morning."

Wanda placed a cup of coffee in front of her. She thanked the woman, then took a careful sip.

"You're out awfully early this morning," Wanda remarked.

Thankful for a reason to look away from him, Margo said, "I guess I am. I didn't see any other guests on my way here to the bunkhouse."

"Ms. Kelsey is probably getting an early start back to Durango this morning," D.B. said, wondering if his voice sounded as flat as he felt.

Margo breathed deeply and tried her best to appear casual, even though her heart was tripping all over itself.

"Actually, I'm not in a hurry at all. In fact, I wanted to speak to you about staying a few extra days."

His brown eyes narrowing with suspicion, he pushed himself away from the cabinet he'd been leaning against. "Wanda, would you leave the two of us alone for a few minutes?"

The redhead shot him an annoyed look. "I've got biscuits baking. Anyway, the woman just said she wanted to stay a few more days. Tell her she's welcome and be done with it."

"Wanda, this is personal," he said warningly .

"No, it isn't personal." Margo quickly spoke up. "I've simply decided that I'd like to spend some time here in the quiet, clean air before I go back to L.A."

"See, D.B.," Wanda said smugly. "She ain't saying anything I don't already know."

D.B. couldn't believe this. Why did Margo want to stay on the ranch? She'd already had her say about his father's will. And he'd already given her his answer. Or maybe she'd had time to think and had decided the two of them should take up where they'd left off in the barn last night. God, if that were so, how could he ever resist her? Would he even want to resist?

Walking over to the table, he looked down at her. "And just when did you come to this decision?"

Margo clutched her coffee cup with a fierce grip, while telling herself she couldn't let him know she was shaking, that the sight of him was making everything they'd shared last night in the barn flash through her mind like some wild, erotic fantasy trip.

"Uh, last night, after I spoke to your father." At least that much was the truth, she thought.

A mocking smile lifted one corner of his mouth. "And I'll just bet he didn't have a thing to do with you deciding to stay."

How could she still want to make love to this man? she wondered, as her eyes roamed over his rugged features. From the day she'd set foot on this ranch, he'd set out to insult her. And even now, she doubted that their heated embrace last night had meant anything to him. So why had it meant something to her?

"Actually, he did have something to do with it," she told him. "He said things were pretty quiet back there and that it would be all right for me to take a few extra days off."

If anything, D.B. looked more skeptical. "I've given you my answer, Margo. You'll be wasting your time to stay here," he said, his voice low and unbending.

Margo shouldn't have been surprised that he still wanted her to leave. But a foolish part of her had thought that maybe after last night, after they'd come so close to making love, he might feel differently toward her. He might even want to spend more time with her. What an idiotic thought that had been.

Trying to ignore the strange little pain coursing through her breast, she said, "Of course I've gotten your answer and I appreciate your feelings on the matter. My staying has nothing to do with—'' She glanced at Wanda then back at D.B. ''Well, I simply want to enjoy being on a dude ranch. I've never been on one before, you know.''

D.B. cut his eyes over to Wanda, who wasn't trying to hide her interest in the conversation. ''Don't you have something to do?'' he asked sharply.

''Not at the moment,'' the cook said, then went over to Margo and laid an arm around her shoulders. ''I think it's grand you want to stay on the Spur for a few days. Havin' a high-powered job like yours and livin' in a big city—well, you need the chance for some peace and quiet once in a while.''

Margo was genuinely touched by Wanda's enthusiasm. ''Thank you, Wanda. And you're right. My life gets very hectic at times. I think it would be nice to slow down for a few days,'' she said, then realized with a surprise, that she truly meant it.

''Maybe I should remind you both that all the cabins are full,'' D.B. spoke up.

''I know you don't have an extra cabin available,'' Margo told him. ''But I'll gladly pay you extra for the bedroom in the ranch house.''

''There's no need for that, Margo. You can bunk with me in my little room off the kitchen,'' Wanda quickly offered. ''I'm usually in here anyway. You'd have the place to yourself.''

D.B. suddenly had the feeling he'd lost all control. But where Margo was concerned, he wasn't quite sure he'd had any in the first place. ''Margo's already settled in the ranch house,'' he said with grim resignation. ''She can stay where she is.''

D.B. looked as though he'd just been sentenced to ninety days in jail. Did he really want to get rid of her that badly? Margo wondered.

She met his dark eyes, then quickly glanced away. "Thank you, D.B. I'll try not to be a bother."

D.B. groaned inwardly. Who was she kidding? Just looking at her beautiful face bothered him. Having her in his house a few more days was going to be sheer torture.

"I'm sure I won't even know you're around," he said dryly.

Margo was making a big mistake. If she had any sense at all, she'd explain the second stipulation of George's will to D.B., then leave this place before her emotions became tangled up with this man.

But Lord help her, she couldn't tell him. He already believed his father was heartless and manipulative. What would he think if he knew his father was willing to pay him if he'd produce an heir?

A vague smile on her face, she said, "Maybe I'll be able to take a good impression of Colorado back with me after all."

A timer suddenly buzzed on the oven. Wanda hurried to shut it off. "Biscuits are ready," she announced. "I'd better go see about the tables."

Relieved that Wanda was finally out of the room, D.B. jerked out a chair directly across from Margo and flung himself into it. "What are you trying to do to me?" he gritted.

Margo couldn't think, much less speak as he leaned toward her, his face hovering just a breath away from hers. "I, uh, what do you mean?"

His nostrils flared as his eyes left her blue ones to travel down her nose and settle on her lips. "You know what I mean. You're not up here to play cowgirl. You're up here to work on my mind—or my body. After last night I'm not sure which one."

Margo sucked in a fierce breath. "You think I had to come all the way to Colorado to find a man to make love to me?"

"I don't know. Did you?"

The question should have insulted Margo, but in actuality it scared her. To think of all the men back in L.A. who'd pursued her, who'd wined and dined her, given her expensive gifts and promised her the moon in an effort to woo her into their bedrooms. None of them had come close to succeeding. But this man with his sardonic looks and sharp tongue had kissed her once and she'd gone up in flames. She'd come close to giving herself to him on a pile of hay! Had she lost her mind?

Her eyes fell from his face and landed on his hands, which were splayed upon the tabletop. "I'm here simply to convey a legal message, not to play with your mind—or anything else," she muttered, her cheeks crimson.

Tense seconds passed and he didn't make a reply. Frustrated by his silence, she looked up at him and was immediately knocked sideways. She'd expected to find mockery on his face; instead she saw something akin to longing.

"Why did you run from me last night?" he whispered.

Afraid her voice was going to fail her, she swallowed desperately. "I—I'm sorry about that. But I think we both know it would have been a mistake if I hadn't."

His hand reached up and closed gently around her throat. Margo began to tremble and she knew he could feel the telltale throb of her heart against his fingertips.

"A mistake?" he whispered, a crooked curve to his lips. "It didn't feel like a mistake when we kissed. Did it?"

No! It had been pure, sweet magic. And she'd never wanted it to stop. But to take up where they'd left off last night would be taking a step to ruination. D.B. only wanted sex. That was pretty obvious to Margo. And she? Well, she didn't want any man in her life.

"No, it didn't feel like a mistake," she said, her eyes unable to meet his. "But just because something feels good doesn't mean it's good for you."

The muscles in his face relaxed and then he laughed just under his breath. In spite of everything, the sound pleased Margo and made her wonder just how many other women had put a smile on his face.

"I'll try to remember that," D.B. murmured. Then he slid his hand daringly down her throat and farther still, until finally his fingers were resting between her breasts.

Margo's breath caught, then shuddered past her parted lips. Why was he doing this to her? And why was she letting him? Margo wondered desperately.

She was telling herself she had to find the strength to get up and away from him, when footsteps sounded behind her, announcing Wanda's return to the kitchen.

Moving abruptly away from her, D.B. leaned back in his chair and folded his arms across his chest. As though he'd been doing nothing more than discussing the weather. Margo, on the other hand, gripped her coffee cup and tried to get her breathing back on an even keel.

"The guests are finally straying in," Wanda said to the two of them. "Breakfast is about five minutes away."

Margo jumped up from the table. "Great! I'll go find the twins and see if they'd like some company."

Wanda watched Margo scurry out of the kitchen, then turned a dubious look on D.B. "Guess you just lost out to two scrawny teenagers."

Not bothering to glance at the older woman, D.B. shoved himself away from the table. "I'm not vying for Margo's attention. I've got better things to do than spend my time entertaining a lady lawyer."

With a loud snort, Wanda turned to pick up a tray of cups and saucers. "Well, I'm sure glad you set me straight on that. I was just about to decide you liked that woman."

After breakfast, Margo found herself strolling toward the stables with Willis holding on to her right arm and Weston the left. The sun had crested over the mountaintop to spread warm, golden bands of light over the ranch yard. The sky overhead was an incredible azure blue and the faint breeze from the southwest carried the crisp scent of spruce.

Margo breathed in deeply and decided there were far less pleasant places to be than here on the Spur. So it didn't have sand and surf. But the snowcapped mountains were beautiful. It didn't have nightclubs or fine restaurants, but she'd never seen people enjoy eating and dancing as much as those last night in the bunkhouse.

A week ago, she couldn't have imagined herself in this rustic environment, much less liking it. She enjoyed the luxury of living in a nice condominium, having a Jaguar parked in the driveway to take her to a shopping mall, a museum or a theater. Anywhere she wanted to go.

But Margo was beginning to think that she didn't really need all that to make her happy. And she blamed D.B. for that. Last night his kisses had stirred her passion, but his words had shaken her very sense of purpose.

If you think your high-powered job and the money it gives you will always keep you happy, then I really feel sorry for you.

Long after she'd gone to bed, Margo had thought about what he'd said. And the more she thought, the more she began to question her motives for becoming a lawyer in the first place. She'd always told herself it was for the challenge, that making a legal maneuver that could either make or break a company was the ultimate thrill. But in the back of her mind she knew she pushed herself at her job because she never wanted her life to be as it had been in her childhood.

Money, or so she'd always believed, could give her everything she'd missed while growing up: clothes, cars, jewels, a house. But in the end it hadn't given her what she'd truly wanted. A father, a family full of love, a home where joy and laughter filled each room.

No, the money she earned hadn't given her that. And she was realistic enough to know it never would. Still, she wasn't about to follow in her mother's footsteps and look to a man for the answer.

"Gee, Margo, it's great you're gonna stay longer," Weston said as the three of them walked along. "Roundup starts today and you'll love that."

"Yeah, that's always fun," Willis added, "and Mr. Barlow says there's at least fifty or sixty head of new calves out there to be hunted out of the brush."

Margo planted her heels in the ground. "Whoa now, guys. I didn't say anything about riding today. I only said I'd come down here to the stables to look at your horses."

Both twins looked crestfallen. "But, Margo," Weston wailed, "you can't miss roundup. It's the big event."

For once Willis wasn't arguing with his twin. "That's right, Margo. No cowboy worth a grain of salt would lay off at roundup time!"

"But I'm not a cowboy," she argued. "I'm not even a cowgirl. I'm a lawyer."

The twins exchanged smug looks. "That doesn't matter," they said in unison.

She laughed. "You two might not think so, but I'm just now getting my legs back from yesterday's outing."

Weston, with his twin's help, tugged her forward toward the stables. "To get in shape you have to keep riding. Besides, you don't want to miss the camp out and eating off the chuck wagon."

"Camping out?" Margo planted her feet once again, causing the twins to trip and nearly drag her down with them.

"No! No camping out for me, boys. I want a real mattress and pillow, instead of the hard ground and a saddle. And I certainly don't want to be a meal for some hungry bear or coyote! So if roundup means camping overnight, then count me out."

"Too rough for a corporate cowgirl?"

Margo's head whipped around to see D.B. A halter was thrown over his shoulder and a feed bucket swung from his hand. He was giving her one of those cocky, challenging looks that made her blood boil.

"I didn't say that."

"That's what it sounded like to me," D.B. drawled.

"Margo's tough enough," Weston quickly defended her, then promptly nudged a finger in her rib cage. "Tell him, Margo. Tell him you can do it."

"Well—yes, I could," she said haltingly. "But I don't know if I really want to."

"Hmm," D.B. said with exaggerated bewilderment. "And earlier this morning you were telling me you wanted to stay and experience being on a dude ranch. I'm beginning to wonder about your wants, Ms. Kelsey."

What could she say without making herself look like an idiot? Nothing, Margo realized. She'd set herself up for this by deciding to stay on the ranch. And she was staying because she had the slim hope that if she could get to know D.B. better, learn what he was really all about, then perhaps she would have a chance of making him see his father in a different light.

"Well, I wouldn't want you to hurt yourself with all that wondering," she told D.B., then glanced at the twins. "Okay, guys, you win. I guess I should see what a roundup is all about."

The teenagers shouted and danced around her. Above their heads, Margo met D.B.'s taunting look.

"You don't have to prove anything to me," he said.

A wan smile crossed her face. "No. But maybe I need to prove it to myself," she told him.

After last night, D.B. knew it was impossible to try to figure what was in Margo Kelsey's mind. He didn't try now. "If that's the case, you'd better head back to the house and pack whatever you'll need for tonight. We'll be leaving in half an hour.''

''Hurry, Margo!'' Willis urged. ''And don't worry, we won't let a bear get you.''

Margo nearly laughed as she headed back to the house. Her meeting up with a bear couldn't be half as dangerous as being alone with D.B. Last night had certainly proved that!

By midafternoon Margo had learned what a roundup was but she still hadn't figured out why she'd agreed to come on one. She was a city person, for Pete's sake. And after yesterday's grueling ride, she didn't think she'd be able to straddle another saddle, much less ride into the mountains, hunting cows and calves.

But here she was, trailing along beside the twins, a bedroll tied onto the back of her saddle and a sense of dread pressing on her shoulders.

It had been one thing to decide to stay on the ranch, but riding out here on the range was entirely another. What was she trying to prove? That she could do all the things the other guests were doing? That she could be a real rootin'-tootin' cowgirl?

Who was she kidding? She'd come on this roundup because of D.B. To show him she could handle anything he threw her way, including his sexy body.

Because they were riding on a valley floor, it wasn't necessary to keep the horses single file. Most of the pack had fanned out in groups of two or three while D.B. meandered his way from the front to the back, stopping here and there to have a word with the guests.

When he reined in beside Margo, she drew her shoulders up straighter and pushed her tangled hair behind her ears. No doubt she looked a mess, but she wasn't in a boardroom now, she was in a totally different element.

"How's the corporate cowgirl? Needing a rest?"

To her surprise, he didn't sound goading or sardonic and she looked at him keenly, wondering what to make of his changed attitude. "Actually, I'm making it very well. Much better than yesterday."

Which was the truth, Margo realized. After she'd ridden for about ten or fifteen minutes, the soreness had begun to leave her. Ringo was acting like an old trusted friend, and the trail wasn't so treacherous that she had to watch every step the horse took.

"I'm glad to hear it," he said, his gaze dipping lazily from her face all the way to the tip of those outrageous black boots. They were scuffed now and caked with dirt and horse manure. Her hair was windblown, her sleeves rolled up to her elbows and a sheen of perspiration covered her flushed face. This Margo Kelsey, he realized, was far more dangerous to him than that prim businesswoman. He could have easily distanced himself from that woman, but this woman, who was gamely falling into his way of life, was beginning to get to a part of him he'd thought was long dead.

"We only have about thirty minutes more riding," he told her, "before we get to a stand of old corrals. That's where we'll drive the cattle to."

"I don't know anything about driving cattle," she told him.

"You don't have to know. Just hang close to me and I'll show you."

She'd hung close to him last night, and look what that had almost gotten her into. Just thinking about it left a track of sweat rolling between her breasts.

"I don't want to be a nuisance to you."

"The other night when you drove up and laid down on that Jeep horn, you were being a nuisance," he said, "but you're not being one now."

Mild surprise lifted her brows as she looked at him. "I don't know if you've just said something nice to me, or if you're trying to be tacky."

He grinned at her. "You think I can't be nice?"

Not to her! Not without some underlying motive behind it, she thought warily. "I know what you can be," she told him. "Sarcastic, hateful, suspicious and cynical." And terribly exciting, she wanted to add, but didn't.

"Now you've offended me," he said to her, but the look on his face said he wasn't the least bit offended.

"I doubt it. Your hide is as tough as Ringo's here." She patted the horse's sleek red neck, something she was beginning to do quite often. Margo had never had a pet before. While growing up, she and her mother had moved too often and had been too poor to have allowed Margo a pet. She'd never realized until now that an animal, even a big one like Ringo, could draw warmth and affection from her and could give it back in return.

"Ringo doesn't have a tough side," D.B. contradicted, "although when he first came to the ranch, he had a tough heart. Like I told you yesterday, he got his name for being an outlaw."

Margo pulled her fingers through the horse's long mane. "He doesn't act like an outlaw to me." She defended her mount.

"No. He soon learned we weren't going to beat or abuse him. Now he trusts me to take care of him."

Margo studied D.B.'s face, which was partially shaded by his black Stetson. He looked like a man who trusted no one. And as for his heart, she doubted anyone had ever touched it.

To the left of her, the twins were engaged in one of their highly animated conversations. Margo glanced at them then back at D.B. "I'd like to thank you again for allowing me to stay on the ranch. Especially after pushing myself on you the other night."

His mouth twisted to a smug line. "Don't kid yourself, Margo. No one pushes anything on me unless I allow it."

He wasn't bragging, merely stating a fact, and Margo could only wonder if George knew that his son was not only strong-minded, he was a man unto himself.

"I can certainly believe that."

Her words seemed to amuse him. Laughing, he touched his finger to the brim of his hat, then nudged the paint with his spurs.

As Margo watched him ride away, a strange wistfulness filled her, a longing that had nothing to do with sex and everything to do with the heart.

Dear God, Margo, she silently pleaded with herself, don't go falling for the man. He was exactly what she didn't need in her life.

Yet she had to admit to herself that he was everything she wanted.

Chapter Six

Once the riders had reached the corrals, groups of twos and threes fanned out and began to comb the valley and the bottom shelves of the surrounding mountains for stray cows and calves.

Margo did as D.B. suggested and hung as close as she could to him. Which wasn't an easy feat considering they were riding in and out of swift streams of water, up and down steep, rocky slopes and into thick stands of spruce and aspen.

Several times she saw him looking back, making sure she was okay and still following. Once, when she and Ringo had managed to climb a particularly steep gully, he even gave her a thumbs-up signal. The acknowledgment had warmed her and made her more determined than ever to hang on until the very last cow was searched out of the brush. For some crazy reason, she wanted D.B. to be proud of her. She wanted him to see that she wasn't just a businesswoman whose main objective in life was to make money.

"You drive this one in," D.B. told Margo much later that afternoon as they headed a little black steer up a gravelly draw.

Wiping a hand across her sweaty brow, Margo darted a nervous glance his way. "Me drive it?" she squeaked. "I'm just a follower."

D.B. shook his head at her. "You can do it. Just keep him in front of you. If he takes off to the left or right, rein Ringo in the same direction. The horse will know what to do."

Fearing the worst, Margo said, "He'll run from me!"

D.B. chuckled at the anxious expression on her face. "He won't. He's too tired. But if he does, I'll be here to help you."

She let out a breath of relief, then told herself she must be going off her rocker. So what if she couldn't get a steer to walk to a rickety old pen a quarter of a mile away? None of this would mean anything once she got back to California. Or would it?

Margo didn't have time to ponder the question. Nor did she want to. She didn't want to think about going back to California. Crazy or not, she was beginning to like it here. And she was beginning to like D.B. California could wait. At least a little while longer.

"This is so far away from the corporate business world," Margo said to him as they urged the steer on down the mountainside. "I can't believe that one day you just said you wanted to be a cowboy and did it. Where did this part of your life come from?"

D.B. lifted his hat and ran a hand over his damp hair. "My mother was a Texan. Born and raised on a huge ranch just west of Austin. My father met her in Dallas, where he'd been working at a brokerage firm." A wan smile touched his mouth as he glanced over at Margo. "She's the one who named me D.B. She thought it was a perfect name for a Texas rancher."

"Is that what she wanted you to be?" Margo asked curiously.

He shrugged. "In the beginning. But after we moved to the West Coast, my father worked hard to change her. He did his best to take the country out of her. And she let him, I guess, because she loved him."

Margo was surprised at D.B.'s disclosure. She'd never heard George speak of his late wife or in-laws. She certainly wouldn't have guessed they were a ranching family. "Your father mentioned you had an uncle in the racehorse business, but he didn't say anything about your mother or grandparents. Or that they were ranching people."

A shuttered look fell over D.B.'s face. "No. I don't expect George would. He tried to keep that part of the family a secret. I think he considered it a sign of bad breeding."

D.B. had insisted that Margo didn't really know George Barlow. At the time she'd believed that had simply been his bitterness talking. Now she was having second thoughts. Since she'd been on the Spur, she was beginning to see a wider view of the whole Barlow family, and what she saw told her that George loved his son, but he'd put conditions on that love. Conditions that D.B. couldn't abide.

"So your grandfather was a rancher," she mused aloud. "Did you always want to follow in his footsteps?"

He looked at her with mild surprise. "My father hasn't told you much about me, has he?"

Not the things that really counted, Margo realized. "Only about your work at the firm and how much he wants you back there."

"Yeah. That's the only important thing to George. The firm. It always came before my mother, me, everything," he said with bitter resignation.

They'd reached the meadow that stretched across the valley floor, making the traveling smoother. Margo carefully kept her eyes on the steer who was plodding docilely along in front of them. "Did you ever want to be a CPA? I mean, really want it?"

When he didn't answer immediately, she glanced over to see him shaking his head.

"I was always good at mathematics and I like working with numbers. But I didn't want to devote my whole life to it. None of that mattered though when the time came for me to attend college. Mother fell in with anything my father wanted. He said being an accountant would be a much more respectable profession than being a dirty cow pusher and that if I wanted my life to count for anything I'd follow his advice."

Margo was saddened by the whole image D.B. was painting of his father. "If he told you that," she said grimly, "he was wrong."

He laughed mockingly. "And what do you consider wrong? The part about the dirty cow pusher, or following his advice?"

"A bit of both," she said truthfully.

He laughed again, but this time he sounded more amused than bitter. "You mean you're actually conceding that my father could be wrong? Maybe I'd better come over there and feel your brow. You must be feverish."

She tossed him an annoyed look. "I never said George was perfect. I said he loved you. And that's something I hate to see you throw away."

"And why would you care if I'm loved or not?"

There was something in his voice, a hollowness that touched her heart and made it impossible for her eyes to remain on his. "Everybody needs to feel loved," she said quietly.

For long moments, the only thing to be heard was the clink of bits and the creak of leather, the breeze rustling the aspen leaves and the distant lowing of cattle. Normally, Margo would have been lulled by the sounds, but as the seconds continued to tick by, every nerve in her body grew tighter and tighter. Was he ever going to say something? Anything?

"Does that include you?" he finally asked.

Margo darted a look at him, then fastened her gaze on the bridle reins she was gripping with both hands. "I suppose so," she told him. "In spite of everything you hear about lawyers, we are humans, with real feelings."

D.B. had never thought for one minute that Margo lacked feelings. When he'd held her in his arms, kissed her, she'd responded with a passion that had threatened to block out every ounce of common sense he possessed. No, she had plenty of feelings, he thought. She was just afraid to show them.

"So I wonder who loves you, Margo Kelsey?"

The question took her aback. For long seconds she stared at him, her mind reverting to the past, then zooming into the future. Who had ever loved her? And who, if anyone, would love her next year, and the year beyond that?

"My mother loves me," she said, unaware of how forlorn she sounded.

"Is that all? Just your mother?"

Numbed by the realization, she nodded. "I don't have any other family. Except your father. He—he's sort of a fill-in dad for me. And I think he feels something akin to love for me."

Her admission stunned him. When he looked at Margo he saw a woman who should be surrounded by a loving family. Instead, she was basically alone. But then so was he.

"Well, at least you have someone. You're doing better than me," he said, his voice vacant.

Margo looked over to see him tugging the brim of his hat down on his forehead. There was an empty look on his face, an expression that said he'd always been alone and never expected to be anything else.

Suddenly there was a lump in Margo's throat, making it impossible for her to say anything. Up until a few days ago, she'd thought of her life as full and successful. But now D.B. was making her question herself and everything she'd ever valued. What good were her law degree, her job, her nice condominium if no one was around to love her?

Once all the stray cattle were rounded up and prodded into the wooden corrals, D.B., several ranch hands and some of the male guests went to work, vaccinating the animals for diseases and branding their hips for identification.

Margo sat on the fence, watching it all from a distance. Several of the women sat nearby, politely including her in their conversation. But since their talk was centered around husbands and children, Margo felt like the odd duck in a flock of geese.

She didn't have any stories about wedding anniversaries, or the birth of a baby. She didn't have a husband that neglected to mow the lawn, but always took her out on Friday nights. She didn't have a child who carried his kitten to school with him in his book satchel, nor did she have nosy in-laws who thought they knew best about potty training a toddler. All of these things were foreign to Margo.

She'd been an only child so she knew nothing about babies or what it was like to have a sibling. She didn't even know what it was like to have nosy in-laws. And the more she listened to these women, the more she thought about the things D.B. had asked her and about her life in general.

She could tell these women what it was like to be in a courtroom, to attend power lunches, to sit in a boardroom full of company executives and give legal advice that could ultimately affect hundreds of people. But that was work. What could Margo tell these women about playing, laughing, and more important, loving?

That question continued to play in her head, until finally, from across the corrals, the twins yelled and motioned for her to join them. Glad for anything that would break the strange mood coming over her, Margo excused herself and left her perch on the fence.

As she neared the spot where the twins were working, Weston called to her. "Come watch us brand."

"Yeah," Willis seconded his brother's invitation. "You've probably never seen this done before."

Laughing, Margo leaned against the corral and looked at the boys through a space between the weathered railings. Dust was billowing up from the cattle's restless hooves and blowing straight in her direction. She waved a hand in front of her face in a feeble attempt to clear the air.

"Until today I'd never seen a cow. At least not in person," she told the twins.

"Gee, imagine that!" Weston said with awed disbelief.

"I thought everybody had seen a cow before," Willis interjected.

D.B., who was standing a few yards away, pulled a hot branding iron from the fire and walked to where the twins had bulldogged a little white-faced calf.

"Not everyone has the opportunity to see or be around animals, boys," D.B. told the twins. "Margo isn't a freak just because she hasn't seen a cow before."

Margo was touched and surprised to hear D.B. defend her in such a way. She would have never expected it from him. Especially since he seemed to resent the kind of life she led back in California.

"Aw, D.B., we weren't putting Margo down," Willis explained. "Anyway, she couldn't be a freak 'cause she's too beautiful."

"Yeah, listen to Romeo here," Weston said, playfully nudging his brother's knee with the toe of his boot.

D.B. lifted the iron from the calf's hip, then glanced over at Margo. She met his gaze and he grinned at her, then looked back at the identically matched brothers. "I guess you two boys are smart after all. You obviously know a beautiful woman when you see one."

He thought she was beautiful? Like this? Amazed, Margo glanced down at her grubby shirt and jeans, then reached up to touch her disheveled hair. She'd never thought of herself as beautiful. She might be attractive and maybe even pretty. But only when she was groomed for work. Only when she was wearing a nice, tailored suit, her hair brushed to a smooth page boy and makeup carefully applied to her face.

"Come over here, Margo."

She glanced back through the rails to see D.B. motioning for her. Warily she climbed up on the fence.

"Why?" she asked. "I might get trampled by a cow if I come in there."

The twins hooted. D.B. merely shook his head and smiled. "You have a bigger chance of being hurt in an earthquake than you do by one of these cows."

Not wanting him or the twins to think she was a coward, Margo climbed over the fence and down into the pen, which was filled with fresh manure.

As she headed across to D.B. and the twins, she kept one wary eye on the cows, and with the other, tried to watch where she stepped.

"I thought you might like to do a little branding," D.B. said when she finally reached them.

"You want me to burn the hair on one of those precious little things? No way!"

D.B. chuckled at her horror-struck expression. "You're not going to kill it, Margo. You're just going to mark its hide."

When her expression didn't change, he caught her by the arm. "Come here. I'll show you it's not that bad. This is just a part of ranch life."

Reluctantly Margo allowed him to lead her over to a small fire on the ground. A couple of irons shaped like a spur were shoved into a bank of red coals. D.B. put the iron he'd just used into the fire then reached for a hot one.

"Get that brindled calf, boys," he told the twins. "That way if Ms. Kelsey ever comes back to the Spur, she'll be able to easily pick it out of the herd."

If she ever came back? Did he honestly think she would? And would he even want her to? she wondered as D.B. led her over to where the twins had downed the calf.

"I really don't want to do this," Margo said in a squeamish little voice. "You go ahead and I'll watch."

"With your eyes closed?"

Annoyed that he was watching her so closely, she glanced up at him. "Is this some sort of initiation ritual? I don't see you asking the other women to brand calves."

Humor grooved a line in his cheek. "This is old everyday stuff to those women. And you did say this morning that you stayed on the ranch to learn more about it. Didn't you?"

She'd stayed on the ranch to learn more about *him*. But how could she tell him that? "Yes, but—"

Before she could say more he pulled her into the circle of his arms. With her back pressed against D.B.'s belly, he put the iron in her hand, then guided it down to the calf's hip.

Margo squeezed her eyes shut and turned her face into D.B.'s chest. His denim shirt was warm against her cheek, the masculine smell of him heady to her senses. Instantly she forgot about the calf as memories of last night swept over her. She'd kissed this man, held on to him as she'd never held on to anyone, and the same urge was assaulting her again.

"Let her up, boys. She's marked with a spur."

Thankfully D.B.'s voice interrupted her runaway thoughts and she looked around to see the calf trotting off to find its mother, seemingly no worse for wear.

Releasing a long breath, Margo stepped out of his arms and away from him.

"Now you can go back and tell my father you're not only a lawyer, you're a real cowgirl."

Looking over her shoulder at him, she scanned his face. "Why don't you come back with me and we'll both tell him?"

The amused look on his face turned sour. "You're wasting your time if you think you can bribe me, Margo."

"That wasn't a bribe," she said through gritted teeth. "It was an invitation. Besides, what do I have to bribe you with?"

His eyes raked insolently from her head to her toes. "Yourself."

Just when she'd started to believe he was a real human being instead of a monster, he had to show his true feathers.

Disappointment filled her eyes and blunted her voice. "You know, I'm beginning to think it's a good thing that you refuse to go back to California. Your father doesn't need a son like you."

Turning on her heel, she stalked back across the pen and this time she didn't even bother to miss the piles of manure.

"You're right about that, Margo. He never needed me. Not one damn bit," D.B. called after her.

His words stabbed her, but she continued to climb the fence, refusing to acknowledge him by looking back over her shoulder. He was a bitter man and she was foolish for ever thinking she could make him see things differently.

The chuck wagon arrived later that evening and by dusk, Wanda and one of the ranch wranglers were serving barbecued beans, beefsteak and biscuits.

To ward off the chilly night air, a big campfire had been built in an open space a few yards away from the chuck wagon. Most of the guests sat in a circle around the blaze, balancing their tin plates on knees or laps. Margo ignored the fire, choosing instead to sit with her back propped against one of the wheels on the chuck wagon.

The twins soon joined her, both of them eating hungrily and chattering happily about the day's goings-on. Margo listened halfheartedly, while wondering what it would be like to be the mother of two boys such as the twins, or simply to be a mother.

In the past years, Margo hadn't thought much about having a child, or a family. She'd never been able to see herself in the role of a wife, or mother. And maybe that was because she'd always been a little afraid to. To her, being a wife and mother meant hardships. Seeing her own mother struggle and suffer through life had taught her that. And look at George, she thought sickly. Having a son had only brought pain and heartache to his life.

Still, when she looked at the twins, at the women sitting around the campfire, who had young children waiting for them back at home, she felt a strange sort of sadness, a void in her heart that she'd never realized was there until today.

Dessert was cherry cobbler. The twins fetched Margo a serving, along with a cup of coffee. She ate tiredly, her gaze drifting often beyond the campfire to where D.B. sat with a group of men.

She hadn't talked to him since they'd tangled in the corral. In fact, it was obvious to Margo that he'd been going out of his way to avoid her.

Well, that was her own fault, she thought glumly. She should have never mentioned going back to California. He'd made it perfectly clear to her what he thought about that idea. But darn it, she had to try, didn't she? After all, that was the reason she'd stayed on the Silver Spur, to eventually get him to change his mind.

But you told D.B. something else. You told him you'd let the matter drop. That you wouldn't bring up George, or the will, or the accounting firm. That you were simply staying here on the Spur to enjoy yourself.

Enjoy herself? Dear God, she was becoming more miserable by the minute and she didn't know what—if anything—could help her. Except maybe a miracle. And Margo didn't believe in those. Only hard work and fortitude had ever gotten her anything.

Chapter Seven

Later, after the last scrap of dessert had been eaten, someone brought out a harmonica and began to play. Soon everyone was crowded around the campfire, singing cowboy songs. Margo joined in on a few, then decided it was a good time to slip down to a nearby stream for a wash.

Thankfully the night was clear with enough moonlight for Margo to find the few toiletries she'd brought among her bedroll and slowly pick her way to the stream.

It was no more than a hundred yards away from camp, down a small gorge, then onto flatter ground where it pooled beneath a heavy stand of aspens.

Margo took her time getting there, especially after she reached the trees, where the leaves cut the moonlight to faint ripples across the ground. The wilderness, coupled with the darkness, made her glance over her shoulder more than once throughout the hike. Margo didn't know what sort of wild animals could be lurking in the forest shadows, and if one was stalking her, she wanted to know about it!

At the pool, Margo carefully sat down on a slab of rock that slanted into the water, then unrolled her pouch of necessities. She brushed her teeth first, then took off her filthy white shirt. The water felt as if it had come straight off ice, and Margo realized it probably had since D.B. had explained to her earlier in the day that all these streams were fed by glaciers of snow high upon the mountains.

The chill of the water as she sponged her skin nearly took her breath away and sent goose bumps shivering across her back and down her arms.

Fearing she would get pneumonia, she washed no farther than the waistband of her jeans, then pulled on a clean striped shirt of thick cotton.

"What the hell are you doing down here?"

The unexpected voice had her whirling around, forgetting that she hadn't yet buttoned her shirt.

"D.B.! I—" She snatched the edges of the shirt together and wrapped them tightly across her breast. "I came down here to wash! What do you think I'm doing?"

He stepped from beneath the canopy of aspen branches and walked over to where she stood precariously balanced on the slanted slab of rock. "Trying to get yourself hurt is what it looks like to me," he growled.

His anger hurt her, and because it did, she lashed back at him. "I hardly think so! What are you doing, playing voyeur?"

Deliberately ignoring her insult, he said, "That water is frigid and you're not used to a cold climate. What if you slipped off that rock and fell in? If I hadn't seen you head off in this direction, no one would have known where to look for you!"

She frowned at him. "You don't have to worry, D.B. Even though I am a lawyer, I wouldn't sue you."

Her words threw D.B. Because frankly, the only thing that mattered to him was her well-being. And it surprised him that she couldn't see that. "I have insurance," he said bitingly, then as he noticed she was shivering, he reached for the buttons on her shirt. "Damn it, the temperature will dip into the thirties tonight. Haven't you heard of hypothermia?"

As he worked to fasten her buttons, she wanted to slap his hands away. But by the time his fingers reached the one between her breasts, she suddenly felt too sluggish to lift an arm, much less drag herself away from him.

"It's June," she reminded him, though she was struggling to keep her teeth from chattering. "People don't get hypothermia in the summertime."

He looked down his nose at her, then felt a surge of unwanted desire flare up in him. Her face was tilted up to his and kissed with the soft glow of moonlight, allowing him to see the soft blue of her eyes, the dusky pink of her lips. She was a temptress and D.B. could only wonder how much longer he could resist her. Or even if he could. "Up here they can. Not to mention being attacked by a bear."

Margo's eyes were suddenly wide. "A bear! You implied there weren't any bears up here," she said accusingly, while unconsciously inching closer to him.

"None have been sighted on the ranch, but it would be foolish to dismiss the possibility of one being near."

"Oh," she said with a sigh of relief, then a grimace quickly tightened her face. "So you think I was foolish for coming down here—alone?"

The corners of his mouth cocked upward, giving Margo her answer.

"Well, I'm sorry," she told him. "No one told me the rules around here. I'm a city girl, remember? Even though I have branded a calf," she couldn't help but add.

As D.B. looked down at her, felt the brush of her body against his, he knew he couldn't stay angry with her. This afternoon, when she'd mentioned his going back to California with her, she'd only confirmed what he'd suspected all along. She was staying on the Spur because of George. She was staying because somewhere in that beautiful head of hers, she thought she could somehow change his mind. D.B. could only wonder how she planned to do it.

He didn't say anything so Margo used the pause in conversation to lean down and retrieve her toiletries and dirty shirt from the rock.

When she straightened, he said, "I guess I'm sorry, too."

She looked at him and her heart began to pound at the expression on his face. It was a look that was both hungry and rueful, one that said he'd been hurt and he wanted her to understand.

"You're sorry? For what, allowing me to stay on the ranch and come on roundup with you?"

No. D.B. wasn't sorry about that. In fact, he couldn't deny that he'd enjoyed having her ride along beside him, answering her questions about the cattle, and simply showing her that part of his life he loved. Moreover, D.B. realized she'd been working extra hard to fit in. And even though she was doing it for reasons he didn't like, he was still endeared by her tenacity, her gameness to meet a challenge that would make some women swoon.

"Look, Margo, I know you're still here because of my father's wishes. You think if you'll hang around long enough you'll make me feel guilty and—"

"I told you this morning—"

"You told me a crock of bull this morning."

Her brows shot upward. "If you thought that, then why did you let me stay?"

His teeth suddenly gleamed white against his dark face. Margo was so mesmerized by the sight, she didn't notice his hand until it was already cupped around her chin.

"Maybe I'm just a sucker for a pretty face."

His fingers were rough, but their touch so very gentle. As Margo stood there looking up at him, she felt her knees go as soft as putty.

"I don't think you could be suckered by anyone. Particularly a woman," she murmured.

The twist to his mouth was both bitter and woeful. "Maybe I'd like for you to think I'm a man of steel, but I'm not."

His hand slid to her throat and the feel of it there, so warm and intimate, had Margo wishing that he hadn't buttoned her shirt, and that his hand had continued its downward trek until it had found her breast.

"What does that mean?" she asked, her voice quavering.

"It means that I'm not inhuman. I do—" His hand eased along the neckline of her shirt, until his forefinger was resting against the shallow indention between her breasts. "Feel things."

If he was feeling the same thing she was feeling, then they were both in deep trouble, Margo thought, as a rush of hot desire swept over her.

"Yes," she said, her voice falling to a whisper, "but do you feel those 'things' with your hands, or your heart?"

Suddenly he was chuckling. "I like it when you make me laugh, Margo Kelsey." He rested his forehead against hers. "I don't know why. But I do."

Bit by bit, Margo was learning that D.B. hadn't always been a happy man. She wasn't really sure that he was happy now. So to know that she could make him laugh and smile, even just for a moment, touched her in a place deep down, a place that was dangerously close to her heart.

"So do you still think I'm using myself as a bribe?"

Funny, but he'd never thought Margo was capable of seducing him just for George's sake. Not that it wouldn't be exhilarating to be made love to by Margo. Dear God, just being this close to her was making his body beg for relief. No, he'd lashed out at her this afternoon, because he'd been angry at himself.

"I shouldn't have said that," he murmured, pressing his lips against her brow. "But I—"

Something in his voice made her lean back enough to look in his face. "But what?" she asked softly, her eyes encouraging him to go on.

He looked at her for long moments, then heaving out a long breath, he led her off the rock and over to a fallen log.

"I think I should tell you something," he said, urging her to take a seat on the weatherworn timber.

He sounded ominous, especially when only moments ago he'd been laughing. "What about? A woman?"

His eyes narrowed suspiciously as he took a seat close beside her. "What makes you think that?"

This time Margo chuckled. "D.B.! I don't imagine you've lived a life of celibacy. And we were discussing me, using my—myself as a bribe. Did some woman actually do that to you?"

"No. I—" He scanned her face. "My father hasn't mentioned a woman to you?"

Her lips parted with amazement. Did he really think she had discussed such things with his father? "No! I've told you the extent of our conversations about you. Why should he mention a woman?"

The bitterness on his face was suddenly so deep and real that Margo outwardly shivered.

"Why should he?" he echoed mockingly. "Well, that's exactly what you need to know, Margo."

"I do?"

There was such an innocent, bewildered look on her face, that D.B. suddenly realized that Margo really was a pawn, maybe even another bribe, although an unknowing one, in the game his father continued to play with him.

"I think you should know that I was engaged for a time. Back before I left the firm."

Like the sharp tines of a pitchfork, jealousy stabbed right through her. "You...were going to get married?"

She sounded incredulous, as though the idea was unbelievable to her. Now that D.B. looked back on it, he could hardly believe it himself.

"Yes. For a while that was the plan."

"What happened?" she asked. Then her eyes widened with speculation. "Your father interfered? Is that why you—"

"No," he said, swiftly cutting her off. "The trouble between Roxanne and I started, well, it started because of me."

Roxanne. The name brought a sour taste to Margo's tongue. "Did you love her?"

D.B. frowned at the question. "Why do women always want to know about love?"

Margo's eyes held on to his. "Because it's all we really care about."

Suddenly he was laughing, loudly. Margo wanted to slap him.

"You find that amusing?" she asked, the flare of her nostrils telling him exactly how much he'd offended her.

"In this particular case," he answered, his laughter quickly sobering. "You see, it turned out that the last thing Roxanne was concerned about was love."

Margo couldn't imagine D.B. marrying such a cold-blooded woman. "What was she concerned about?"

"Money. Appearances. Money. Social life. Money. You get the picture, don't you?"

She got the picture all too well, and it sickened her. Nodding glumly, she said, "I take it you found this out after you were engaged?"

He shrugged. "I knew from the beginning that Roxanne liked the high life. But so did everybody else I knew back in Santa Monica. I mean, that's what it was all about. Work yourself to death, so you can keep up with the rest of the fools."

He looked down at the toe of his boot, then slowly a smile spread across his face as he realized that Roxanne's defection didn't matter anymore. In fact, he was beginning to see that the only thing she'd hurt was his ego. Certainly not his heart.

"It wasn't until later," he went on, "when we began discussing our future plans that things went haywire. I guess you could say she had a fit of the vapors when I told her I didn't plan to stay with the firm. That I wanted to try my hand at ranching."

Margo's face mirrored complete surprise. "You mean, you'd planned all along to leave the firm? That it wasn't something done in the heat of anger?"

D.B. shook his head. "Not hardly. Like I told you earlier, it wasn't my idea to become a CPA, but I did because my father wanted it so badly. And I foolishly went along because I wanted to please him." With a self-deprecating snort, he looked at Margo. "I spent the first thirty years of my life trying to please my father, to gain his respect, his love. I didn't realize—until it was almost too late—that I was losing myself in the process."

Dear Lord, Margo, what have you gotten yourself into? D.B. wasn't just a son wanting to spite his father. He was a man trying to be himself, make his own identity. And he deserved to be happy. She wanted him to be happy! So what was she going to do now?

D.B. laughed again, but this time the sound held no bitterness. Rather it was a sound of pure relief, making Margo look to him for an explanation.

"Hell," he said, "I guess I should mail Roxanne a thank-you card for opening my eyes."

Margo started to ask him if he still loved the woman, but stopped the words before they could leave her tongue. It wasn't her business if he still loved her. Besides, D.B. might get the wrong idea. He might even think she was beginning to care about him. And that was something that would never do. She couldn't let herself care about D. B. Barlow.

"So where does your father fit in with you and Roxanne? If he didn't interfere—"

"Oh, he interfered all right," D.B. interjected. "After the engagement was broken. Good ole Dad went to Roxanne and offered her an exorbitant amount of money to patch things up with me. I guess he had the notion that if he couldn't persuade me to stay in Santa Monica, Roxanne could."

Margo could only stare at him as she tried to imagine how he must have felt, knowing his father had literally tried to buy back his fiancée for him. And George... What had the man been thinking? She knew he loved D.B., but to go that far was more than insulting, it was crazy!

Slowly she shook her head. "I'm so sorry, D.B. I didn't know." She let out a heavy sigh. "Your father only told me that you two had disagreed over your leaving the firm. If I had known about all this other— well, I doubt I would have agreed to come up here."

Maybe it was a good thing she hadn't known, D.B. thought. Otherwise, he might not have ever seen her, held her in his arms, kissed her lips. But he couldn't tell her that. She wasn't a woman he could be having second thoughts about. She was a career woman who belonged back in his old life. Not here in the mountains.

"Well, now you know why I accused you of being a bribe."

"So what about Roxanne and the money? How did you find out about it? Surely George didn't tell you!"

He let out a short laugh. "I knew something was strange when she came to me, begging to put our engagement back together. When I confronted her for reasons why, she finally confessed to taking my father's money."

By now, anything D.B. told her shouldn't come as a shock. But it did. How could any woman do such a thing? Especially to a man like D.B.? And how, now that Margo knew all this, was she going to be able to tell D.B. about the second stipulation of his father's will?

Before she could think of a reply, D.B. reached for her hand and pulled her to her feet. "We'd better be getting back to camp before everyone comes searching for us."

Impulsively, Margo laid her hand on his forearm. The touch had D.B. glancing quizzically down to where she was holding on to him, then back up to her face.

"D.B., I'm glad you told me all this. And for what it's worth, I think you have every justification for being bitter and angry. But—there's one thing it doesn't change."

"What is that?"

"That your father needs you."

D.B. shook his head in wry disbelief. "You never give up, do you?"

"I never have . . . yet."

"So what makes you think my father needs me? Because his heart is bad?"

"No," she said matter-of-factly, "because you're his son."

Long seconds ticked by without him saying anything and from the remote look on his face, she didn't expect him to. Disappointed, Margo stepped away from him and started walking back up the trail to the campground.

* * *

Margo couldn't sleep. For the past three hours she'd tossed back and forth in the narrow sleeping bag, squeezed her eyes shut and commanded herself to sleep. When that hadn't worked, she'd stared into the dying flames of the campfire some distance away and prayed for sleep to come. That hadn't worked, either. So now she was getting up. Maybe if she walked around for a bit, it would relax her enough to let her eventually get to sleep.

Since she was already wearing clothes, she unzipped the sleeping bag and reached for her jacket, which was lying next to her. The night air had become quite cold, making a white mist rise from the slightly warmer ground.

It shrouded the mounds of sleeping bags scattered here and there around the camp. But from what Margo could see, no one was having trouble sleeping... except her.

D.B. heard Margo the moment she got up. In fact, from where he lay, he was able to see her bedroll, and earlier, he'd watched her tossing and turning. She was obviously troubled about something and D.B. wished fervently that he didn't care.

From the corner of his eye, he watched her tiptoe quietly past the chuck wagon, then on past the campfire. But the moment she disappeared into the edge of the forest, D.B. reached for his boots. What was the woman doing, going on a nature call?

He'd give her five minutes. If she didn't reappear by then, he was going after her. And this time he'd make sure she understood the dangers of wandering off!

* * *

Margo ambled through the edge of the forest, then decided to cross the meadow to where the horses were penned in the corrals. The cattle had been let loose earlier in the evening, and probably wouldn't be seen again, the twins had told her, until the fall when another roundup would occur and part of the herd would be hauled to market.

By then Margo would be back in California at her desk in a high-rise office building and far away from horses and cattle. And D.B. But she'd be thinking about him and this place. She probably always would.

D.B. felt a strange sense of relief when he finally spotted Margo at the corrals. Ringo was stretching his neck over the railing, vying for her attention, and she was obliging with gentle pats on his nose.

As D.B. grew nearer he could hear her saying to the horse, "Ringo, you and I are more alike than you think. We're both loners."

The melancholy sound in her voice made D.B. pause some few yards away from her. She was describing herself as a loner! How could that be? The woman was successful and beautiful!

The horse nudged the side of Margo's head and neck with his nose, making a wan smile touch her face. "Oh, I know there are other horses around here to keep you company. I have lots of people around me, too. But neither one of us has someone special. Someone who really loves us."

Incredibly, Ringo's head pumped up and down as though he understood and agreed with Margo. Rubbing him fondly between the ears, she crooned, "If I didn't live in a city, I'd take you home with me. And then we'd always have each other.''

Too struck to move, D.B. continued to stand in the shadows just out of Margo's sight. A lump was in his throat and he cursed himself for being so soft. She was only talking to a damned horse, but her words were from the heart. And they told him that she was far from the woman he'd first imagined her to be. She wasn't just a cool, corporate lawyer with lots of ambition and very little feelings. She was a woman who needed and wanted to be loved.

Still, he couldn't make himself step forward and make his presence known to her. He was afraid to. He was afraid that he would be tempted to take her in his arms and assure her that she wasn't really alone, as she thought. And there was someone who loved her. He did.

No! That couldn't be right, he countered fiercely. He didn't love Margo. Did he? He just wanted her to be happy. But wanting a person to be happy didn't necessarily mean he loved her. Did it?

The questions tore through D.B.'s head, tugging his heart first one way and then the other. Until finally he decided the best thing he could do for both of them was to go back to camp and try to forget he'd heard her say anything.

Chapter Eight

The next day, the trip back to the ranch seemed docile to Margo after the rough-and-tumble adventure in the mountain brush. But by the time they rode up to the ranch yard, she was exhausted. Not necessarily from the physical demands of the roundup, but rather, from her lack of sleep last night.

Even so, she made the ride easily and was inwardly proud of herself because she knew she was growing physically stronger every day.

After handing over Ringo to a wrangler's care, she headed to the house for a long hot bath. Once she was freshened up, she went to the phone, intent on calling George.

However, what could she say to the man? D.B. hadn't changed his mind.

Groaning wearily, she punched out the numbers anyway, then waited for the housekeeper to get him on the line.

"Margo! You can't imagine how anxious I've been for your call," he said before she had the chance to speak.

Margo sank onto the edge of the bed. "I'm glad to hear you sounding more rested. Are you feeling all right? Has Grace been taking good care of you?"

"Don't waste time on me and Grace," he said quickly. "I want to hear about D.B. Have you made any headway with him?"

Actually she had, Margo thought. He'd opened up to her. And she'd learned more about his life than she ever expected to know. But as for getting him back to California, the prospects looked dismal, and she might as well let George know it.

"I'm afraid not, George. And frankly, I'm not so sure—"

"What?" he urged when she hesitated.

She sighed. "I'm not so sure D.B. should go back to Santa Monica. He loves it here, George. This is the kind of life his mother came from. The type of life she initially wanted for D.B. Why didn't you tell me that before?"

The older man spluttered as though he couldn't believe Margo was asking him such a thing. "Because I didn't think it was important for you to know. That life isn't what D.B. wants. The boy doesn't know what he wants!"

Things were becoming more and more clear to Margo. Especially now that she'd heard D.B.'s side of the story. "D.B. isn't a boy, George. He's a grown man."

"Well, he's *my* boy. But I guess he'd like to change that, too," he said with glum resignation.

Tiredly, Margo pushed her damp hair away from her face. "No. I think D.B. loves you very much. He just doesn't approve of your attitude—or the things you do."

There was a pause, then, "I believe I hear accusation in your voice."

His voice was laced with surprise and hurt. Margo felt awful, but knew she couldn't avoid the truth. "I'm not accusing you of anything, George. But I am wondering why you didn't tell me about Roxanne. You know that was a big factor in the reason D.B. cut himself off from you."

Long seconds passed. Margo was beginning to think he was going to hang up on her.

"George?"

The older man sighed heavily in Margo's ear. "Listen, Margo, that whole thing with Roxanne—it wasn't something D.B. should have gotten so angry over. I thought he wanted her back, so that's what I tried to do. Get her back for him. Hell, I was only doing it because I loved him and wanted him to be happy!"

Strangely enough, Margo believed George's desire was to make his son happy. Still, that didn't justify the tactics he'd used to do it. "George! You tried to buy your son a wife! Do you know how insulting and degrading that would be for any man?"

"Well, it sounds to me like you've gone over to the other side. What has D.B. been telling you anyway?"

"The truth," she said grimly, then let out a heavy breath. "George, you know that I didn't just come here as your lawyer. I came because you're very dear to me and I'd like more than anything for you to have a good relationship with your son. But you've got to understand that I'm caught between the two of you. And I don't like it!"

"Well, you don't have to be caught between us," he said sharply.

"What do you mean?"

"Have you told D.B. that I want a grandchild? That I want this family to have an heir to carry on the name?"

Margo closed her eyes. "No! And I think it would be a mistake to tell him about that part of the will. In fact, I think you should take it out completely. He already thinks you're trying to buy him back into your life."

George cursed loudly. "Hell, Margo, the boy is right. I am trying to buy him back. It's all I know how to do."

A terrible sadness swept through Margo, because she knew that George was telling the truth. He was a man who knew all about making money, but very little about loving.

"Listen, Margo," he went on firmly. "You tell D.B. about the second part of the will, then come on home."

"George—"

"Now don't argue with me. I understand it's not right for me to put you in the middle of this thing. Just tell him to get busy with getting me a grandchild and then you'll be out of the picture. We'll consider your job there finished."

Margo was suddenly frozen by his words. She'd never be totally out of the picture. She'd never be able to separate herself from George or D.B. George was her boss and friend, a part of her everyday life. And D.B. wasn't just the name of George's son anymore. He was a real man that she'd come to know and . . . love?

Shaken by the question, she mumbled to George that he was probably right and that she'd be heading home soon.

She wasn't even aware that she'd hung up the phone until a few minutes later when a knock sounded on her bedroom door.

Drawing a few deep breaths to collect herself, Margo went to open the door. As she suspected, D.B. was on the other side, his face freshly shaven, his dark hair damp and combed back from his forehead. He looked incredibly handsome, and her heart twisted to a painful knot in her chest.

How could she tell D.B. that his father was willing to pay him millions of dollars to produce a grandchild for him? He might just be tempted to do it, she thought wildly. After all, he wouldn't have to have any contact with George. He wouldn't have to go back to California. No, all he would have to have was a willing woman. And for a man like D.B., she wouldn't be hard to find.

But what kind of woman would she be? Would she really love D.B. and his child? Or would she be like Roxanne, more concerned about the money? Margo shuddered at the thought. She couldn't bear to think about him being hurt twice in the same way.

"I thought I'd better check and see if you'd collapsed in here," he said. "You looked pretty tired when we got back to the stables."

She nodded, inwardly surprised that he'd noticed. "I was. I didn't get much sleep last night."

D.B.'s eyes gently roamed her face and the curtain of blond hair falling close to her eye. "I know."

Her brows arched quizzically. "You do?"

Realizing he'd spoken the two words aloud, he cleared his throat and said, "Well, you can't be used to sleeping outdoors on the hard ground."

He was right. But that wasn't the thing that had kept her awake. He had. Last night, after their talk at the stream, she couldn't get him, or what he'd told her, out of her mind. And the more she thought, the more it dawned on her that she was becoming too emotionally involved with D.B.

But she didn't know what to do about it. Or if it was already too late to stop this unexplainable longing she felt every time she came near him.

With a brief smile, she said, "I'm not used to it. Can you imagine sleeping outside in Santa Monica? There probably wouldn't be any chance of suffering from hypothermia, but there would be plenty of other dangers to worry about. And not one of them would be bears."

Smiling back at her, he said, "I hope you never try it. Dad might lose his lawyer."

"George is resourceful. He'd find another one." She tried her best to joke.

But not one like you, D.B. thought.

"Dinner is only about an hour or so away," he said. "I thought if you were still tired, I could bring yours to you. That way, you wouldn't have to go back down to the bunkhouse."

His thoughtfulness came as such a surprise that she could only stare at him, her lips parted.

"Well," he said with annoyance when she failed to answer. "Would you like that, or not?"

"I—" She shook her head. "Uh, no. I've rested now. I'll come down to the bunkhouse. But thank you for asking."

"Fine," he said, somewhat embarrassed now for making the gesture. She was looking at him as if he'd lost his senses. And perhaps he had, D.B. thought. Because all he could think about as he looked at her tanned face with its soft full lips and powdery blue eyes was that he wanted her. He wanted to step over the threshold and into her bedroom. Shut the door and the world away from them. Then slowly make love to her until he was so exhausted, his mind would cease to think about the right or wrong of it.

D.B. looked uncomfortable, but not nearly as awkward as Margo felt. Something about the way he was looking at her was altogether different. She was seeing a soft, gentler D.B. and the sight left her warm, shaky and confused.

"I'll see you down at the bunkhouse," she told him.

Nodding, he forced himself to step back before his body could talk his mind into something he'd later regret.

At supper Margo sat across the table from D.B. As he'd come to expect, the twins flanked her, but though they vied for her attention, Margo remained rather quiet throughout the meal.

D.B. didn't know what was preoccupying her thoughts. But he damn sure knew what was possessing his. Her. He couldn't keep his mind or his eyes off her. She was wearing a skirt the color of a ripe peach, and a matching cotton sweater that veed deeply at the neckline.

The sight of her smooth, tanned skin reminded him how it had been to touch her face, her throat, her breast, her thighs. Even now he could still taste her lips, hear her soft sigh in his ear.

Yet as his eyes clung to her quiet face, he realized he didn't just want to make physical love to Margo, he wanted to make real love to her. He needed to see a look of utter happiness and contentment on her face and to know that he'd put it there.

Once the evening meal was over, most of the guests gathered for card games. Although the twins begged Margo to stay, she quickly excused herself and walked back to the ranch house. She was tired, and after her talk with George, she felt as if a heavy weight had been slung over her shoulders.

Tonight as she'd eaten her meal, she'd looked at D.B. and realized she couldn't go on anymore. George was right. She needed to get her job over with and go home. Put herself out of the picture.

It would be far better, she told herself, to leave the ranch with a troubled heart than to hang around and eventually leave with a broken one—something Margo was sure would happen if she stayed much longer. D.B. would never be interested in her romantically. And even if he was, their lives were far too different to intertwine.

At the house, Margo went to her bedroom with the intention of lying down. However, once she was in the small confines of the room, she realized she was too restless for that.

There was a television in the living room and someone—she supposed it had been D.B.—had built a fire in the fireplace before they'd gone to supper.

Margo switched on the TV set then took a comfortable seat in a rocker by the fire. There was a documentary on about the Great Depression of the 1930s. Margo was glad to find something interesting enough to hold her attention. Yet midway through the program, as

Margo watched people struggle to find and hold on to the basic necessities of life, one thing kept coming to her mind. Family and loved ones. For most of those people, everything had been stripped away. Money, cars, houses, even clothes and food. Most of them lost their pride and some their dignity. But in the end all that mattered was keeping their family together.

Before she'd come to the Silver Spur, Margo had never questioned the direction she'd chosen to take in life. In fact, she'd grown up determined to get better than what she'd had and to make sure she never lost it. But now she could only ask herself if she was happy. Was she crazy for wanting money and the security it could provide her, or was D.B. crazy for shunning it?

D.B. returned to the house just as the program was ending. Surprised to see him, Margo switched off the television.

"I hope you didn't leave your guests because of me," she told him.

Actually, D.B. had left the bunkhouse because Margo wasn't there. And he wanted to be with her. No matter that his common sense told him to do otherwise.

Walking over to where she sat in the rocker, he turned his back to the warmth of the fire. "The guests don't need me around to keep them entertained," he assured her.

He was no more than a foot away from her. To have his tall, dark face looming over her, set Margo's heart into fast forward.

"I've been watching television," she told him. "A documentary about the depression era."

D.B. reached for a poker, then pushed at the burning logs. "You think if I'd watched it, I would reconsider accepting my father's will?"

His voice held more amusement than anything and that annoyed Margo. "Not really," she quipped. "You don't strike me as a man that can be impressed to change his mind. Even if he knows someone is suffering. Besides," she added more gently, "the depression taught us more than what it's like to do without money."

He stashed away the poker, then turned to her, his brows arched quizzically. "You think so?"

She nodded. "It taught people all about priorities and made them see what was really most important to their lives."

D.B. took a seat on the elevated rock hearth and crossed his booted feet out in front of him. "So what did you learn, Margo? Did seeing all that hardship and suffering make you want to hurry back to Santa Monica and earn every dime you can?"

She frowned at him. "You would think that of me," she said dully.

He hadn't really meant to insult her, but something inside D.B. made him want to goad her, to make her realize that she, not necessarily him, needed to take a second look at priorities.

"I'm sorry, Margo. I just wonder about you."

Her heart went a little faster as her eyes lifted and clung to his. "You wonder about me?"

D.B. folded his arms across his chest—mainly to keep from reaching out and hauling her onto his lap. "Does your mother live near you?"

Margo let out a short, caustic laugh. "I've offered many times to set her up in a nice apartment near me. But she says she's happy with her latest husband."

"Have you ever thought that maybe she *is* happy with him?"

Margo shook her head. "I don't know how she could be happy. All they have to live on is his Social Security check and what little she makes waitressing."

"Maybe that's all they need to be happy." He reached over and took her hand, then gently pressed it between the two of his. "You know, Margo, it isn't necessarily weird or wrong for a person to be content with less."

As she studied his face, the depth of his serious brown eyes, she asked herself if she'd been wrong all these years. Had she been wrong for placing so much importance on ambition and less on the people who were close to her?

"I, uh, think I should tell you something," she said to him.

Something in her voice made everything inside him go suddenly still. "What?"

She drew in a deep breath then let it out slowly. "I talked to your father this evening."

His fingers tightened on hers. "Is he all right?"

The concern on D.B.'s face made it even more difficult to go on. But she had to. She had to get this all over with. She had to get away from this man before she fell deeply and irrevocably in love with him.

"Yes. In fact, he sounded much stronger than the last time I spoke with him."

Relief crossed his face. Margo went on before she lost her courage. "He wanted me to... tell you something."

D.B.'s eyes suddenly narrowed. "What now?"

"Something about the will."

He groaned loud and long. "Damn it, Margo, I've already heard all I want to hear about that will."

She felt utterly sick inside. "Not this part."

D.B. shook his head. "If there's more, just keep it to yourself. I think you know me well enough now to know it won't make a difference with anything."

Slipping her hand from between his, Margo rose to her feet. "It might," she said lowly.

He snorted. "So why didn't you tell me earlier? Why did you wait until now?"

"Because I didn't want to tell you!" she burst out, feeling more frustrated than she'd ever felt in her life. "I kept thinking you'd change your mind and say you'd be willing to go back to California and the firm."

"You were wrong," he muttered.

How well she knew that. "Yes. Well, I've come to see the light, D.B. You were right about many things. One, being that your father will do lots of manipulating to get what he wants."

Realizing that it had cost Margo to say that, D.B. reached out and touched her shoulder. Immediately her eyes swept up to his. They were full of sadness and regret and something else he was afraid to read.

"I know my father means a great deal to you. Hell, he means a lot to me, even if I can't live around him, or even be around him. But I'm glad you realize he isn't perfect."

Hope suddenly dawned on Margo's face. "If you realize the man isn't perfect, then couldn't you forgive him? Don't you want to be with him before the years pass and it's too late?"

D.B. shook his head with resignation. "Believe me, Margo, for years I tried to have a normal father-son relationship with George. He wouldn't allow it. He always had to be in control of everything. My job, my friends, even my fiancée, for God's sake! I'd be a damn fool to go back to that."

"I agree. You shouldn't go back to that. You shouldn't go back until you're ready to stand up to your father."

D.B. cursed loudly. "Just what in hell do you think I've been doing the past three years?"

"Hiding from him."

Anger shot through D.B. like a crippling bullet. "I've heard enough!"

He started across the room toward the hallway. Margo rushed after him and grabbed a hold of his arm. D.B. turned and glared at her, but she refused to let his mood intimidate her. She had to finish this. Once and for all.

"No. You haven't heard enough," she said in a rushed voice. "Your father wants you to produce an heir."

There. It was out. It was over. Margo could leave and forget she'd ever met this man.

D.B. stared at her as if she'd just invited him to go to the moon. "He what!"

The words burst from him, making Margo unconsciously step backward. "You heard right. Your father wants a grandchild. And if you produce one within the next three years you'll stand to inherit several million dollars."

His brown eyes turned a furious black.

"And you think I'd be interested in such a cold-blooded proposition?" he flung at her.

Margo could no longer look him in the face. It was too painful. "D.B., just take a moment and try to look at this from your father's point of view. He feels as if he's lost you. He'd at least like a grandson to carry on his name."

D.B.'s face turned so hard, Margo would have sworn it had been chipped from stone.

"Are you crazy, woman? Take a look around you," he invited with an angry sweep of his arm. "Do I look like a family man? Do you see a wife in this house—just waiting to have my child?"

Margo wasn't afraid to face D.B.'s ire. But the relief she felt at knowing there was no other woman around put a fearful lump in her throat. Dear God, how could she want this man without a heart? "No. I don't see a woman. But I—"

In the space of a second, his eyes widened then narrowed to slits of angry speculation. "Oh, I think I'm getting it now. You're telling me all this because you want to offer yourself as the mother!"

When she said nothing, D.B. reached for her shoulders. Margo winced as he gave her a little shake. "Tell me! I'm right, aren't I?"

Stunned beyond words, Margo continued to stare at him. Dropping his hands, as though he considered touching her filthy, he glowered back at her.

"Don't bother answering!" he spat. "It's pretty damn obvious you'd like to give George a grandson. My God, he'd probably give *you* the whole firm. And that's what you really want, isn't it? That's what you've been after all along!"

Fury rushed through her, staining her cheeks with a furious red and curling her hands into tight little fists. "You're the one who's crazy, D.B.! If you think I came to this ranch to be impregnated by a swine like you—"

Her words were cut off as he jerked her up against him, then captured her chin between his thumb and forefinger, forcing her to meet his gaze. "I think it's exactly why you're here. You're no different than Roxanne. She was willing to marry me for my money. Now you're willing to have my baby for it!''

With all the strength she could muster, Margo whacked her palm against his jaw. The unexpected blow surprised him and caused him to loosen his grip on her. Margo wasted no time in backing away from him.

"I'm not willing to bear you anything, D. B. Barlow! Not now! Not ever!'' she said in a low furious voice.

His eyes bored into hers, as absently, he rubbed a hand against his stinging jaw. "We'll see. Won't we?''

Margo answered his hateful taunt by spinning on her heel and running out of the room.

By the time Margo was inside her bedroom, she was shaking all over and tears were streaming down her face.

How could D.B. think such things of her, much less say them to her? The accusations he'd hurled at her might as well have been stones. They'd certainly hurt just as badly.

She went to the bathroom, washed her face with cold water, then studied her image in the medicine chest mirror.

What was wrong with her? Why did D.B. have the power to hurt her so? She'd been insulted by men before. Some had accused her of being cold, others had called her unfeeling and not needing anyone but herself.

None of what they'd said had affected her. She'd been determined not to let it. So why did it matter what D.B. thought of her?

Fresh tears spilled over her eyes and she wiped at them desperately. Crying was a weakness she couldn't afford. But dear God, how could D.B. think she was so greedy, so calculating, that she would bring an innocent child into the world for money—it was beyond bearing!

And where did he get the idea anyway? she thought furiously, as she bent her head and splashed more cold water onto her face. She'd never come on to him. Never implied that she wanted to go to bed with him.

But you have been thinking it, Margo. Every time he's touched you, each time he's near, you think about making love to the man.

The little voice running through her head caused her to grip the edge of the vanity. Yes, she could admit that she wanted to make love to the man. But did that mean she wanted to go as far as to have his child?

Weakly, she pushed away from the vanity and walked back out to the bedroom. On the north wall was a wide window covered with heavy drapes. Margo went to it and pulled the curtains enough to allow her a view of the dark night.

From this angle, she could see one end of the bunkhouse and farther below it, a portion of the horse stables. Here and there a yard light illuminated the little cabins and corrals standing off in the distance.

It was strange, Margo thought, how familiar the place had become to her and how differently she viewed the Silver Spur than when she'd first seen it.

Margo had discovered a lot of things during the past few days. She'd learned that luxuries were just that and nothing more. That she could actually ride a horse for long distances and still remain friends with him. She could dance and sing and even have fun in the crudest of surroundings.

But more than all that, Margo had come to realize her life in Santa Monica wasn't really as full and happy as she wanted to believe. D.B. had made her see that she needed more than a career. She needed a family of her own. Someone to love her. Someone she could love back.

But did all that mean she wanted to have his child? Dear God, yes. If D.B. really loved her, giving him a child would be wonderful. If he really loved her, she believed she could forget all about California and live here in these remote mountains.

Hot tears began to ooze from her eyes once again and she turned away from the window, just as in her heart she turned away from the image of her and D.B. as a family. D.B. didn't love her. In fact, right about now he probably hated her.

Chapter Nine

D.B. had come to the stables hoping to find some sort of relief for his tortured thoughts, yet as he walked down the wide alleyway between the rows of horses, he realized he'd come to the wrong place.

Everywhere he looked brought back memories of the night he and Margo had stood in this very place and kissed as though they had really wanted, even loved, each other. Had she been trying to seduce him then? he wondered. Had she already planned to try to get pregnant with his child?

The idea saddened and angered him, and oddly enough, even excited him. To make love to Margo, to put his child in her belly, was not a repulsive image. In fact, it would be the most wonderful thing that could happen to his life. If—oh yes, *if* she was doing it out of real love.

With a tortured shake of his head, he propped his fist on top of a stall gate. Before Margo had come to the ranch, he'd believed himself to be happy. He'd thought he'd put California, his father and Roxanne—*everything*—behind him. But now he wondered if Margo could be right. Was he hiding from his father? Had he ever really faced up to him?

Oh, he'd argued with his father and he'd avoided him. And hearing Margo talk about George had made D.B. realize how much he'd missed the old man. But then Margo had made him realize a lot of things. Mainly that he didn't want to live the rest of his life alone.

Wearily, he leaned his forehead against his fist and closed his eyes. He didn't want to live without a woman's love. He didn't want to go through life without having children and a family. But he damned well didn't need his father buying him one.

Deciding the barn was not the place to be, D.B. left the horses and walked over to the bunkhouse. He found the card games still going and Wanda in the kitchen preparing another tray of snacks.

"Well, look at you," Wanda said with surprise. "I thought you'd retired for the night."

D.B. grunted and walked over to the coffeepot. "I had to check on something down at the barn," he said.

Wiping her hands on her apron, Wanda studied his dour expression. "Must have been something bad. You look like a grizzly bear that's just been stung by a mess of honey bees."

He'd been stung all right, D.B. thought grimly.

"What makes you say that? There's not a thing wrong with me."

"Yeah. And I was Miss USA back in '65. Gravity does a lot to a woman in that length of time."

Muttering a curse, D.B. walked over to the cook. "You think you're a smart old woman, don't you?"

Wanda laughed. "Would you have hired me if I wasn't?"

Deliberately ignoring the question, D.B. lifted crackers and cheese from the tray. "How have the games been going? No arguments, I hope."

Wanda shook her head. "No. Everybody in this group seems to get along well. Even the twins are behaving tonight. 'Course that's probably because Margo isn't around. They'd both stand on their heads to get her attention."

"You're not telling me anything I don't know," he said gruffly, then yanked a chair out from the kitchen table.

Wanda watched him straddle the piece of wooden furniture as though he'd rather be breaking it, instead of sitting on it. "By the way, where is Margo?" she asked him.

D.B. scowled. "How should I know?"

Annoyed by his attitude, Wanda picked up the tray and swept past him. At the door she paused and said dryly, "Oh, I don't know. But since she's *your* guest, staying in *your* house, I just thought *you* would be the person to ask."

Feeling awful, and hating himself because he did, D.B. groaned and scrubbed his face with both hands. "Wanda, the woman came here for money."

Wanda, who'd been about to go out the door, jerked her head around. "What did you say?"

"I said money, damn it! Margo is after money."

Forgetting the snacks and the guests, Wanda hurried back into the room and plopped the tray down on the table where D.B. sat hunched over the back of the chair. "I don't believe you. Where did you get such an idea?"

D.B. shook his head. He didn't like admitting it to Wanda any more than he did to himself. "From her," he said in a low, pained voice. "She and my father have cooked up this legal thing together."

Wanda dismissed his words with a quick wave of her hand. "From what I hear, your pa don't need money. And from the looks of her, Margo doesn't, either."

D.B.'s laugh was bitter. "Wanda, you're one of the normal people in this world. You don't know how it is with people who have money, like my father, or even Margo. They always want more."

Seeing he was really serious, Wanda took a seat across the table from him. "D.B., I don't know anything about lawyers or business. And I sure don't know much about money, except that you give me a nice, fair paycheck each week. But I do know a little bit about people. And when I look at Margo, I don't see a money-grubbing woman."

D.B. slanted her a skeptical look. "Maybe you'd better look again."

"No. You're the one who'd better look again. Margo's a lonely woman. I can see it in those pretty blue eyes of hers. She doesn't want money. She wants what most all women want. Love. But I don't guess you could do anything about that, now could you?"

More than two hours later, D.B. entered the house, fully expecting Margo to still be shut up in her bedroom. Instead, she was in the kitchen, wearing a silky blue robe with—from what he could tell—nothing under it.

D.B. stood at the doorway, watching her stand on tiptoe and push things this way and that on the cabinet shelf. With each little movement of her rounded hips, the flimsy material shifted and slid provocatively against her.

The sight was sweet torment to D.B. and it was all he could do to keep from going to her and bending her over the kitchen table. "I figured you were still hiding in your bedroom," he said as he walked farther into the room.

At the sound of his voice, Margo went suddenly still, then slowly turned to face him. "You're the one who's hiding. Not me."

The robe wrapped in a vee across her breast. D.B.'s eyes followed the neckline, then traveled downward to where the material split against her thigh. She was the most sensual, desirable woman he'd ever seen. And he loved her. He could no longer deny it.

Letting her comment slide, he moved to within a step or two from her. "Were you looking for something in particular?"

She nodded. "Aspirin. I've developed a headache."

He crossed the room, to a smaller cabinet above the microwave. After a moment of searching, he pulled down a bottle filled with white tablets. "Maybe you should eat something. You barely touched your supper."

She was surprised that he'd noticed her lack of appetite and even more shocked by his obvious change in moods. A few hours earlier, he'd been in a furious uproar, accusing her of all sorts of things. Now he seemed almost contrite.

"I'm not really hungry," she said.

He shook out two of the aspirin, then handed them to her with a glass of cold water. Margo swallowed the pills, then placed the glass on the cabinet behind him. When she turned back around he was still there beside her and she felt completely naked as his eyes roamed over her bare face and tear-reddened eyes.

"I'd like for you to eat something anyway," he said, his voice dropping to a murmur.

Margo looked at him, her expression full of hurt and confusion. "Why are you worried about me, the greedy bitch?"

"I didn't call you that."

She swallowed at the lump filling her throat. "You might as well have."

Wanda was right, he thought. Margo's eyes were full of pain and longing. Why had he just now recognized it?

Moving closer, D.B. touched her forehead, then pushed his fingers into her soft blond hair. "I'm sorry, Margo. Now that I—I've thought about it, I know I was wrong about you."

Her heart wanted to believe him, but common sense told her she'd be a fool to take his words, or the gentle touch of his hand, seriously. "I'm the same woman you were shouting accusations at earlier tonight. Why should you think any differently now?"

His hand left her hair to cup the side of her face. It was all Margo could do to keep from closing her eyes and turning her lips into his palm.

"Because," he said, "the past few days you've been trying your best to talk me into going back to California to see my father rather than trying to talk me into bed with you."

Her heart thudding heavily, she lifted her eyes from the front of his shirt up to his face. "So why didn't you think about that a few hours ago?"

It was obvious to D.B. that she wasn't going to make this easy for him. But hell, he thought, nothing had been easy from the first night he'd laid eyes on her.

"Because, damn it, Roxanne fell for one of my father's offers, I figured you had, too." He shook his head, his expression rueful. "But hell, you coming up here, planning to get pregnant with my child—it's ludicrous now that I think about it. You're a lawyer, a businesswoman. You'd never want to be a mother, not even for money."

That was exactly what Margo had been telling herself for years. All she had to depend on was herself and all she had to watch out for was herself. It was safer that way. No broken hearts, no broken dreams. Just her and nothing else. So why was her heart aching to reach out to this man? Why would she give all of herself just to be a part of his life? Because she loved him. Madly, unwisely, but totally.

"Or would you?"

The question came so softly, Margo wasn't quite sure she heard it, then when it dawned on her that she had, she froze.

"Would I what? What are you saying now, D.B.?" she demanded.

Seeing she'd taken his question the wrong way, he said hurriedly, "I don't mean—not for money!"

Moving closer still, his hands curved over both her shoulders.

"I simply meant, would you want to have a child?"

She looked at him guardedly. "I never thought much about it until—" Until I met you, she very nearly finished. "Well, I've never had a relationship serious enough to make me consider the question. Why?"

He opened his mouth to answer, then suddenly he muttered something under his breath and turned away from her.

Bewildered, Margo watched him walk across the room, turn, then walk back to her. He stopped just short of touching her, and as she looked up into his brown eyes, her heart began to pound with longing and confusion.

"I want you to marry me, Margo."

Feeling as if someone had whacked her across the knees, Margo reached back and gripped the edge of the cabinet. "Are you—is this some hateful joke?"

D.B. groaned. He knew he was doing this all very badly, but now that he'd started he had to go on. He had to make her understand just how much he needed her.

"No. I'm very serious."

She looked at him, her expression both dazed and vulnerable, and suddenly D.B. could imagine that same look on her face as a child each time her mother had presented her with a new stepfather and promises of a real family. It had never happened, and D.B. knew Margo was still thinking that having a real family would never happen. Not to her.

She laughed, even though the last thing she felt was amused. "Sure. About as serious as going back to California. I don't know what kind of game you're trying to play on me. But it won't work."

He pulled her rigid body against his and wrapped his arms around her. "I'm not playing a game," he murmured next to her ear. "I want you to be my wife."

Margo drew in a shaky breath and with it the musky masculine scent of him. "D.B., you don't even like me."

Like her? He was crazy about her! It was a relief to finally admit it to himself. Laughing at the wonder of it, he put his hands in her hair and drew her face away from his chest. "Why would I want to marry someone I don't even like?" he asked, grinning, his eyes twinkling down at her.

He looked pleased with himself, even happy. Margo could figure none of it out.

"I really don't know. Why don't *you* tell me?"

He laughed again, this time deep in his throat, and brought his lips against hers. "I think it would be better if I showed you," he murmured.

Once he began to kiss her, Margo ceased to think. For the past two days, she'd wanted nothing more than to be in his arms again, to feel his hard, warm body next to hers, to taste the dark excitement of his lips. It didn't matter what he was doing, or why he was doing it. She wanted him. More than anything in her life.

Eagerly, she raised on tiptoe and curled her arms around his neck. As their lips and tongues tasted, their hands explored. Hers slid across his chest, down his arms and around to his back. His touched the slender column of her throat, her stomach, her rib cage, then upward until his fingers came in contact with the mounds of her breasts.

Quickly he pushed aside the flimsy robe and the soft fullness spilled into his hands. Margo moaned in the back of her throat and dug her hands beneath the tails of his shirt until she was touching the smooth warm skin of his back.

Desperately, she pulled him closer, until his hips were grinding into hers, matching the urgent search his tongue was making of her mouth.

"Oh, D.B.," she gasped when his lips finally lifted. "You don't know what you're doing to me." She was on fire. Her need for him thrummed through her body like a runaway engine.

"Yes, I do know," he said thickly as the tip of his tongue circled the edge of her ear. "You've been doing it to me from the first moment I saw you."

"I...can't...believe that," she whispered hoarsely.

"You will," he said. Pushing the robe off her shoulders, he brought his face down to her breast where he brushed his lips lightly against one rosy nipple. "You'll know exactly how much I want you, once we make love."

Once we make love! Something about the smug certainty of those words sent a shot of fear through Margo. Did he want to marry her, make love to her, simply to get her with child? Of course he did! He'd stand to gain millions. That's what this sudden flip of his switch was all about!

"No!" Furious now, she shoved hard against his shoulders.

D.B. raised himself away from her. "Margo?"

For a moment she almost believed the look of love and desire on his face. She almost gave in, tugged his head back down to hers and let consequences be damned. But she couldn't live with herself if she did. And she certainly couldn't live with a man who was simply using her for his own gains. Tears welled up in her eyes and she blinked at them desperately.

"Margo, what's wrong? What do you mean, no? No to getting married? No to having children?"

Infuriated that he could act so guileless, she squeezed out from between him and the cabinet. God, he nearly made her forget there were morals of any kind left in this world!

"Oh, I'm sure you're hoping it's not the question about children," she said in a tightly accusing voice.

His eyes widened as he watched her jerk the front of her robe back together and tighten the sash at the waist.

"I'm hoping it's not about either question," he told her. "I'm thirty-four years old, past the age where most men start building families of their own. But that doesn't mean I want to live the next thirty-four without one."

Margo felt sick and cold and a pain so deep inside her, she was afraid to take a breath for fear it might split her apart.

"Oh, I'm sure of it," she said, purposely keeping her back to him. No way did she want him to see how much he was hurting her. "And I'm sure you came to this conclusion tonight. Some notion out of the blue came to you and told you it was time to start a family."

He crossed the few steps to where she stood, but stopped himself from reaching out for her. "Actually, it did," he said gently. "Or you did, by bringing up the idea of me having a child."

In a few minutes he'd probably be telling her they would get married as soon as possible, have the child, then split the money between them. How could she bear it? "Well, at least you're honest enough to admit that," she said, her voice thick with pain.

D.B. smoothed his hand over the back of her golden hair. "Margo, I understand a woman expects flowers and rings and romance when she's proposed to, but I'm not a wine-and-roses type of guy. I acted out all those games back in California, followed all the traditions and social expectations. It didn't make me happy and in the end it didn't get me married."

Her throat was suddenly aching with a million tears. She didn't need for him to give her wine and roses. Couldn't he see that? She needed something that he'd never be able to give her. True love. "And what would make you happy, D.B.?" she asked, her voice quivering.

Why wouldn't she turn to him, look him in the face, say something that would tell him what she was really thinking? D.B. wondered.

"You."

The simple word shocked her. Spinning around on her heel, she locked gazes with him. "You really expect me to believe that?"

Torment filled his eyes and creased his face. "I know this all seems sudden to you. Hell, it seems sudden to me. But it also feels right." His hands closed around her shoulders, his head bent to hers. "When I kiss you, hold you, it's like—" Breathing deeply, he brought his lips to within an inch of hers. "It's something special. It's something I don't want to give up. Have I been presumptuous in thinking you feel the same way?"

"You tell me."

He closed his eyes as though he was struggling to find the right words to say to her. "Margo, a few minutes ago, when I held you in my arms—I can't believe you were acting."

No, she hadn't been acting then, but she had to act now. She couldn't let D.B. see that she'd been foolish enough to fall in love with him. "And you expect me to believe you're not acting?"

His hands reached up to cradle her face. "I expect you to believe me when I tell you I love you."

The words were like three sharp arrows through the heart. "I wondered when you'd get around to saying that," she said sadly.

His eyes searched her face. "What does that mean?"

"It means that I won't marry you and I certainly won't have your child! It means I think you're the most hypocritical—the biggest corporate shark that's ever walked the face of this earth!"

Whirling away from him, she ran from the room as tears began to pour down her face.

"Margo!"

Ignoring his call, she hurried out to the living room. She had to get away from him. Her heart couldn't stand another lie.

She was about to enter her bedroom when his hand came down on her shoulder like a hot band of steel. "What are you talking about?" he demanded.

Disbelieving laughter and angry tears bubbled up in her throat, then spilled out in the quiet room. "You're going to play innocent right down to the end, aren't you?" she asked bitterly, then followed it with a caustic laugh. "Your father's right. You don't belong on this ranch. I think you belong in New York. With your acting ability you'd be a smash on Broadway."

A dark flush spread across his face as his fingers clamped around her upper arm. "You think I'm lying?"

"Oh, I think you want to marry me. And I think you want me to have your child. But not for the normal reasons."

D.B. couldn't believe she was saying this. A part of him was furious that she could judge him in such a way, while the other part wanted to laugh at the craziness of it.

"Margo, I understand that I hurt you when I accused you of—well, of wanting my father's money, or my money. But at least I had reason to suspect you!"

Her lips quivered as tears threatened to overtake her. "And I have plenty of reasons to suspect you. Several million of them!"

He stared at her in cold silence, then finally released the grip on her arm. "I've obviously made a big mistake about you. I thought you were different. I thought you were the woman I wanted to spend the rest of my life with. Wasn't I the fool? Again!"

Before Margo could say a word, he turned and stalked off. Shaking and furious, she slammed the bedroom door and locked it. No way did she want any more intrusions from D. B. Barlow. Not in her room. And definitely not in her heart.

Chapter Ten

The night was once again a cold one. But this time Margo was prepared. This time she was wearing more than thin silk and flimsy high heels. She'd donned a heavy white sweater over her jeans and pulled on two pairs of socks before tugging on her boots.

Even though the Jeep had a heater, it was not airtight and Margo didn't intend to freeze all the way back to Durango. She was in enough misery without adding to it.

She hadn't been in the Jeep since the night she'd first driven up to the ranch, and she hoped the thing wouldn't give her a problem about starting now. The last thing she wanted was for D.B. to hear the starter grinding and come down to investigate.

Since it was four o'clock in the morning and all the lights were still off in the house, she supposed D.B. was asleep. And that's the way she wanted it to stay. She'd had enough confrontations with him to last her a lifetime. As for saying goodbye to him, well, she knew D.B. probably wouldn't care that she'd avoided the courtesy. No doubt he'd be greatly relieved when he woke up in a couple of hours and discovered she was gone. He'd considered her a nuisance from the start anyway.

After stashing her things in the back, she climbed up behind the wheel. The engine sparked to life almost instantly and she gave a sigh of relief as she released the clutch and turned the vehicle back down the sloping drive.

In order not to wake D.B. or disturb any of the guests, she kept her headlights off until she was away from the house and past the row of cabins. It wasn't until the Jeep rattled over the cattle guard at the entrance that she pulled on the lights. Ahead of her was the road back to Durango and ultimately the way back to California. She thought she'd feel relief at finally being on her way. Instead she felt an overwhelming sadness, an unexplainable grief at leaving the ranch and the man she'd come to love.

And she did still love him. It didn't make sense that she did. But there it was in her heart anyway. She didn't know how long it would take for the feelings she had for him to finally die and fade away. She prayed it would happen soon.

But if the terrible pain in her heart was anything to go by, she knew she was in for a long wait. Like the rest of her life.

For the first time since D.B. had lived on the ranch, he overslept. Not that the fitful tossing and turning he'd been doing could have been called sleep, he thought as he switched on a bedside lamp and fumbled groggily for his wristwatch.

The gray fingers of early dawn had already pushed their way through the curtains on the bedroom window and slanted across the foot of his rumpled bed. Six-thirty! Wanda was already cooking breakfast and he hadn't even been to the stables yet!

With a groan of disbelief, he fell back against the pillows and closed his eyes. This was what a woman did to a man, he thought. She changed his habits, mixed up his head, turned his wants and needs into something altogether different from those he'd started out with.

Opening his eyes, he rolled his head toward the pillow next to him. He could easily picture Margo there. He supposed he'd already imagined her there a hundred times since she'd come to the ranch. This morning, however, the image seemed to be even more vivid and he could see her blond hair like tangled silk against the sheets, her blue eyes drowsy with desire. Just the taste of her dusky pink lips would be worth losing a morning's work over. But was it worth losing his heart over?

Who was he kidding? He'd already lost his heart to Margo. Now he had to figure out what to do about it.

Groaning, he shoved back the covers and headed toward the shower.

The guests were already being served breakfast by the time D.B. made it down to the bunkhouse. Wanda, who was just coming out of the kitchen with a basket of hot biscuits spotted him coming through the door.

Quickly she motioned for him. "What in the world has happened to you two?" she asked frantically. "I thought maybe there'd been a freak gas leak or something and you were both lying up there dead!"

"Both? What do you mean—" Not bothering to finish the question, D.B.'s head swung around and his gaze scanned the crowded tables for a sign of Margo.

"Margo isn't down yet?"

"No," she said, then suddenly grinned as she noticed the haggard lines on his face. "Uh, I guess I'm getting old, D.B. I should have known you and Margo were, uh, well occupied with each other instead of gassed to death."

D.B. shot the older woman an impatient glare. "Wanda, if you think I spent the night with Margo, you're crazier than I thought!"

She laughed. "Since when is it crazy for a man to make love to a woman? Especially one that looks like Margo?"

D.B. wasn't in the mood to argue that point. He hadn't seen Margo, or any sign of her since he'd gotten up this morning. And since the twins were eating alone, she obviously wasn't here in the bunkhouse. So where was she? Still in bed?

Forgetting Wanda, D.B. crossed the room and looked out the window. Her Jeep was gone! When had she left? *Why* had she left?

Turning away from the window, he nearly bumped into Wanda, who'd scurried after him like a nosy puppy.

"What is it, D.B.? Is something wrong?"

He took hold of Wanda's shoulders with both hands. "Margo hasn't been here in the bunkhouse at all this morning?"

Wanda shook her head. "No. But neither have you. That's why I was beginning to worry."

A sinking feeling rushed to the pit of his stomach. "Well, she's gone," he said flatly.

Wanda's brows shot upward. "And she didn't even say goodbye? Well, I—I just can't hardly believe that, D.B. She'd planned on staying awhile." The cook looked sadly at the twins. "Those boys are sure gonna be hurt. Maybe you'd better tell them she's gone."

D.B. nodded, his face like chipped granite. "Yeah. Maybe I'd better tell them. They need to learn to steer clear of women like Margo Kelsey before they're old enough to be hurt by them."

"Like you?"

He turned a bitter look on Wanda. "Don't kid yourself. I'm not about to let a woman hurt me. Not now. Not ever."

"Is she really gone, D.B.? I can't believe she didn't tell us she was going!" Weston exclaimed after D.B. had broken the news to them.

"She's gone," he said flatly and began to fill his plate with scrambled eggs and bacon, even though the last thing he wanted to do was eat.

"But she was planning on staying a few more days," Willis argued with obvious disappointment. "We were going to teach her how to saddle Ringo all by herself."

D.B. ladled gravy over a biscuit, then doused it with black pepper. "Face it, boys. Margo wasn't interested in horses or cattle, or anything about this ranch. She was only leading you boys on."

Completely puzzled by that, Weston frowned. "She didn't have any reason to lead us on. Besides, Margo was getting real good at riding and she was liking it, too. And she loved Ringo."

D.B. whacked off a piece of biscuit with his fork and tried to ignore the pain in his heart. So what if Margo had loved Ringo? She sure as hell hadn't loved D.B. She thought he was a shark, just out for her body and the money it would ultimately produce for him. And as for the ranch, she was probably shouting hallelujah now that she was headed back to the bright lights of L.A.

"This place was boring hicksville to Margo, boys. You should know right now that if you want a woman like her, you've got to..."

He paused, searching for a way to explain without bursting the twins' innocent expectations. Weston and Willis looked at him intently.

"You've got to be nice to her," Weston finally finished for him. "That's what our mom always tells us. Be nice to your girlfriend and she'll like you."

"And you've got to kiss her a lot," Willis added. "Dad says women like to be kissed probably more than anything, 'cause they like to know they're wanted."

"Yeah," Weston quickly seconded. "And you've always got to tell her you love her. That's the most important thing. Dad says you better tell her you love her every day, or she might forget."

D.B. opened his mouth, intent on telling the boys that they had been misinformed. But as he looked from one twin to the other, it dawned on him that these teenagers knew more about loving a woman than he did.

"Sounds like your parents have told you a lot of things."

Willis nodded proudly. "Yep. They want us to be like them when we get married."

"I take it they're happy," D.B. said, reaching for his coffee. Maybe if he drank several cups of caffeine, the muddled feeling in his head would leave. At the moment, he didn't like thinking that he'd grown to be just like his father. Insensitive, cold-blooded, thinking a person's feelings could be bought and bartered. It was no wonder Margo hadn't trusted him.

"As happy as two hogs in a mud hole," Willis answered.

D.B. stared into his coffee cup. Maybe if his parents had been as happy as two hogs in a mud hole, he would have grown up differently. Maybe he wouldn't be afraid to go after Margo and try to convince her once and for all that he loved her.

"Why don't you go after her, D.B.?" Weston suggested. "I'll bet she'd come back if you went after her."

D.B. looked at the teenager. Could the boy be right? Or was he crazy to even hope there could ever be anything between them?

"Yeah. Go after her, D.B." Willis quickly echoed his brother's sentiments. "She made everything fun."

D.B. wiped a hand over his tired face as a war of indecision waged inside him. "I think it's too late for that, boys."

Both twins looked at him, their expressions crestfallen.

"Gee, we're sure gonna miss her," Weston said woefully.

"Do you think she'll come back next summer?" Willis asked hopefully.

No. Margo would never come back, D.B. silently answered. Not unless he went after her. And even then, she still might tell him to go to hell. But so what if she did? Living without her was going to be like hell anyway.

Before the twins knew what was happening, D.B. was on his feet.

"If I have anything to do with it, she's going to come back now. Today," D.B. told them. "You boys tell Wanda where I've gone."

"Yeah! Now you're talkin'!" Weston exclaimed.

"And don't worry," Willis said with a broad grin. "If any problem comes up around here, we'll take care of it."

D.B. affectionately ruffled the top of the twins' heads. "I know you will. Thanks, boys."

Margo stopped for breakfast in Creede, an old mining town built between two slabs of steep, rocky mountains. She parked the Jeep on the narrow main street and walked down the wooden planked sidewalk until she found a café.

It was full of people—mostly men. As Margo stepped inside she decided the place had once been a saloon, probably back when the town had been in its heyday. Indeed, the long bar where she took a seat had more than likely seen its share of whiskey bottles and beer mugs. Even the swinging batwing doors on the front entrance looked as though they'd come straight off the set of "Gunsmoke." Only she knew they hadn't come off a set just to produce an image. This place was for real. As real as the Silver Spur had been.

She ordered pancakes, and as she ate the rich breakfast she wondered how long it would take her body to get back to surviving on a slice of dry toast and a pot of coffee in the morning before she went to work. A week? Two? Whatever it was would be a snap compared to putting her heart back together. D.B. had made such a hash of it, she sincerely doubted it would ever mend.

Several times during the meal, the batwing doors squeaked as they pushed open to let another customer inside. Each time, Margo looked over her shoulder, half expecting to see D.B. sauntering in with spurs on his feet, six-shooters on his hips and a deadly look on his face.

It would be just like him to want one last showdown
with her. To make sure she knew how much he loathed
her. To make sure she knew never to return to the Silver Spur. But he never appeared and she told herself she
was glad even though her eyes were burning with unshed
tears.

Her breakfast over, she walked back to the Jeep. On
the way, she noticed a pay phone on a street corner. The
idea of calling the airport in Durango and reserving a
ticket back to California crossed her mind, but she
shrugged it off.

There was no need to be in that much of a hurry. D.B.
obviously wasn't chasing after her. Indeed, he was
probably sharing a joyous breakfast with the twins right
about now, she thought glumly.

The twins. And Wanda. She hated leaving without
telling any of them goodbye. But at least she knew the
small town where the teenagers lived. She was sure
they'd get a letter if she sent it general delivery. As for
Wanda, Margo supposed she could write to her, too.
But how could she explain her sudden departure to the
older woman or anyone else for that matter? Why
would anyone believe she was stupid enough to fall in
love with a man who'd barely been civil to her?

That wasn't true, a little voice came back at her. A
man had to be far more than civil to kiss a woman the
way he'd kissed her.

Shaking her head, Margo breathed deeply and
climbed back into the Jeep. She couldn't think about
that now. She had a long drive ahead of her, through
mountains that would terrify even the bravest of souls.
She had to keep her wits about her and try to forget that
she'd ever met D. B. Barlow.

* * *

By the time D.B. reached the summit of Wolf Creek Pass he began to doubt he'd ever catch up with Margo. True, she was driving a four-wheel-drive vehicle with a top traveling speed of about fifty, but he had no idea when she'd actually left the ranch. It could have been shortly after he'd gone to bed at midnight, or as late as this morning before daylight.

The whole idea of her slipping off in the dark without a word to anyone both angered and hurt him. Did she hate him, mistrust him that much? He had to be insane for going after her when everything she'd said indicated that she despised him.

But D.B. wasn't going to think of all those heated words they'd flung back and forth at each other. He was only going to think of the way she'd melted in his arms, the hungry way she'd kissed him. She might not have said she loved him, but she'd damn sure acted like it. And right now that was enough to keep him speeding on down the highway.

"Two hours! Are you certain there is no other flight to California before then?" Margo asked the woman behind the counter.

"I'm afraid not, Ms. Kelsey. Perhaps you could do some shopping while you wait. There's several nice boutiques downtown and none of them close before nine."

Margo shook her head. She'd been traveling all day and had already returned the Jeep to the rental agency. All she wanted to do now was get on a plane and put Colorado and D.B. as far behind her as she could get them.

Hefting up her bags, Margo said, "No. I'll just wait here in the terminal. Thank you anyway."

An hour and a half later, she was still waiting. Her head had begun to throb and her stomach, outraged that it had gotten nothing but coffee since the pancakes early this morning, had clenched into a hard burning knot.

Margo knew she should eat before she got on the plane. Even a sack of potato chips from the vending machine would be better than nothing. But she couldn't summon the energy or desire to cross the waiting area to where the snacks and beverages were located. All she wanted to do was to close her eyes and to try and figure out how things between her and D.B. had gotten so close so fast, then just as swiftly had gone awry.

When D.B. spotted her, she was still sitting there with her head tilted back against the seat, her eyes closed, her face pale and lifeless. His heart was suddenly wrenched with pain and longing and he knew that nothing mattered except that she know, really know, how much he loved her.

"Margo?"

Her eyes flew open and for long moments she sat there motionless, staring up at him as though he were an unwelcome vision.

"What are you doing here?" she asked warily.

D.B. stood over her, his eyes drinking in her soft beauty. Why had it taken him so long to realize he loved her? Was he so much like his father that he didn't know real love until it slapped him in the face?

"To stop you."

Her lips thinned. "What's the matter? You didn't find the money I left for you on the kitchen bar?"

"Money? What money?" he asked, his expression clearly muddled.

She raised up on the edge of the seat. "For my room and board these past few days. I told you I'd pay you. If it wasn't enough, I could have mailed you a check. There was no need for you to chase me for a hundred and fifty miles!"

"I didn't come here for money of any sort, Margo. In fact, I'm damned tired of talking about money!"

So he'd come for that final showdown after all, Margo thought, her heart sinking painfully. When she'd first opened her eyes and saw him standing over her, a wild sort of hope had shot through her. For a few ridiculous seconds, she'd actually thought he might be here because he loved her. Silly her!

"Well, I'm damned tired of talking to you—period. Isn't it enough for you to have the last word, or do you have to keep driving it into a person?"

Needing to be closer, he sank down on the cushion next to her. "Why did you sneak out last night without saying anything? Were you afraid to face me?"

Actually Margo *had* been afraid to face him. A part of her had been afraid she'd throw away her pride, tell him she'd marry him for whatever reason.

Her eyes fixed on a spot across the room, she said, "There wasn't anything left to say, D.B., except goodbye. And I hardly think you wanted one of those from me."

In spite of her bitter voice, he took her hand and tenderly cradled it between his. She looked at him, her eyes full of hurt and confusion.

"I want everything from you."

Stunned by the conviction in his voice, she looked down at their tangled fingers. "D.B., I—we don't know each other. All we have going for us is…a healthy dose of lust."

"You're wrong, Margo. I know you feel more than lust for me. Look at me and tell me you don't."

He lifted her chin with his forefinger. As Margo's eyes met his, her lips began to tremble.

"Maybe I do," she whispered. "But I'll get over it."

"Not if I have anything to say about it."

"I won't marry you just so you can give your father a child! I love George and I want him to be happy, but I won't go that far."

Shaking his head, D.B. glanced around to see that several of the waiting travelers were giving them curious looks. He lowered his voice for her ears only. "I don't want you to marry me for George's sake. I want you to marry me, for me. And if you give me a child, I want it to be for me, for us. Not because George wants it."

She made a sound of disbelief. "I'm supposed to believe that? I've only been around you a few short days. And in that length of time you certainly didn't act like a man in love."

His fingers tightened on hers. "Tell me, Margo. How does a man in love act? 'Cause I don't know."

Her nostrils flared as she drew in a shaky breath. "You never told me you loved me. Not until it was suddenly convenient for you."

He wiped a frustrated hand over his face. "I didn't tell you before because I didn't know before!"

"Hmm, it must have whammed you over the head like a hammer. Hit you like a thunderbolt out of the blue."

"At least I was able to admit to my feelings. That's more than I can say for you."

"Maybe you'd better explain that," she said icily.

"I'm not going to explain anything to you with an audience," he muttered, tugging her to her feet.

"My bags!" Margo screeched as he hurried her out the front entrance of the terminal.

"Damn the bags."

It was well past dark now. Street lamps lit the wide parking area. As he led her toward a dark, two-toned pickup, a jet could be heard circling overhead.

"You're going to make me miss my flight," she said to him.

"That was my intention."

"Why?" she demanded.

He opened the pickup door and pushed Margo inside, then skirted around the hood and slid in beside her on the bench seat.

"Because I don't want you to leave. I won't let you leave unless—" With a frustrated groan, he reached for her and clutched her close against him. "Are you afraid to tell me you love me?"

In spite of all her fears and doubts, Margo's hands gripped his shoulders and her face buried into the side of his neck. He felt so good. How could that be?

"Why should I tell you anything? You only want to use me." She raised her head just enough to look at him. "I won't be like my mother, D.B. I won't be gullible and softhearted and believe the first man who comes along with kisses and promises."

Her blue eyes were full of anguish and D.B. suddenly realized she wasn't fighting him, she was fighting herself.

"You'd rather be hard-hearted and alone?"

"At least I won't be deluding myself."

He pushed his fingers into the hair at her temple. "Margo, I'm asking you again. Do you love me?"

She couldn't look at him like this, be in his arms and so close to his heart and tell him a lie. "Yes," she whispered. "I do love you. Is that what your ego needed to hear?"

Suddenly his fingers were on her cheeks, touching her as if she were immeasurably precious to him.

"No. It's what my heart needed to hear," he said gently.

It was the last thing she'd expected him to say and the sweetness of it brought a rush of tears to her eyes. "I want to believe you, D.B. But I'm afraid. Last week I didn't even know you."

"Last week I didn't know what love was," he whispered against her lips. "I don't think I would have ever known if I hadn't met you."

Closing her eyes, she groaned. "Oh, D.B. There's nothing special about me."

"Oh, yes, you are *very* special," he said, opening his mouth over hers.

For a long time he simply kissed her. Over and over. Touching and worshiping her mouth, letting his lips tell her everything his words could not.

Hope unfurled inside Margo like a bright red ribbon and she clung to him and kissed him back with every fiber of her heart.

Eventually he lifted his head and gently stroked her hair off her forehead. "I know this thing between us has happened quickly. And last night I know it probably wasn't the best time to propose to you. But I swear, Margo, my wanting to marry you or have a child with you has nothing to do with my father's will. And to prove it—"

"You don't have to prove it," she began, only to have him shake his head.

"Yes. I don't want anything to stand between us. Now or ever. So if—or when—we have a child, the money will be set aside in a trust fund. Solely for him. Or her. What do you think about that?"

Margo felt as if she'd drunk a gallon of champagne and millions of joyous bubbles were bursting inside her. He loved her. *Really* loved her! A slow, impish grin spread across her face. "I think it could be a him. Or a her. Or maybe a them. Why should we stop with just one baby? We don't want it to be an only child, do we?"

Suddenly he was laughing and holding her so tightly that neither of them could scarcely breathe.

"You are going to marry me," he said surely.

"Yes."

He put her away from him and held the sides of her face with both hands. "I know there're lots of things we still have to work through," he said, his expression quickly sobering. "You have a career in California and—"

"I don't have to have a career," she hurried to assure him. "I know I don't know much about ranching, but I want to learn. And living in the mountains will be all I need as long as you're there."

He shook his head. "No. I'd never ask you to give up what you do. You worked very hard to become a lawyer. I don't want you to sacrifice all that just for me. I can live in the city again. I can even work as a CPA again. Hell, I can do anything, live anywhere, as long as you're with me."

Tears spilled from Margo's eyes. She couldn't believe that anyone could love her that much, could sacrifice so much just to be with her. "Never! Never! I know how much you love the ranch. I couldn't live with myself if you gave it up for me."

As he looked into her eyes, D.B. felt such a deep rush of love, it actually pained him. "My sweet, sweet Margo. I know what it's like to have someone tell me what I should or shouldn't do. I know what it's like to have to put aside the things I really wanted to do and pretend I was happy doing something else."

"Your father," she said with a sad sigh.

He nodded. "I'd rather die than be like him. I'd rather give you up right now than to do to you what he's done to me."

Reaching up, she trailed her fingers across his cheek. "So. What are we going to do?"

"I've been thinking about that a lot," he said, then with a grimace, he shook his head. "No. Who am I kidding? I've been thinking about me and you since the first night you showed up on the ranch. I was angry at myself for wanting you. Especially when I knew you weren't the kind of woman who could fit into my life."

Margo smiled knowingly. "And I've been telling myself I was crazy for wanting a man who despised everything about my life." Her expression grew serious as she locked her fingers at the back of his neck and brought her forehead against his. "But I couldn't stop myself from falling in love with you. Now all that matters to me is that you're happy."

How could he have ever thought Margo a shallow, selfish woman? She was nothing like Roxanne. She was not like any woman. And he loved her! Loved her with that part of himself that he never knew existed until now.

"There's at least six months out of the year that snow piles high against the cabins and makes getting to the bunkhouse and stables a major effort. There's nothing to do during those times, but throw out feed and hay to the cattle and horses. The men working for me can easily handle that job without my being around. We could spend those months in Santa Monica, then live on the Spur during early spring and summer.''

"You'd be willing to do that for me?" she asked, her eyes wide and questioning. "What about your father and the firm?"

He smiled and then his smile turned to laughter. Funny, he thought, how having a mate changed a man's thinking. "It's not going to be a problem for me. It might be for George when he learns I'm going to run the firm the way I want it."

"You've been away a long time," she pointed out.

"Yes. But you were right. It's time I faced up to my father instead of simply avoiding him. I'm my own man now. It's time he knew that."

"He loves you. I know you probably still don't believe that. But he does."

His throat grew thick with emotion. "These past few days with you have taught me that it's not always easy to tell a person you love them, or show them that you care. I realized I was more like my father than I thought."

Margo looked at him hopefully. "Then you can forgive him for the mistakes he's made?"

D.B. nodded. "I believe I already have. But you and I together are going to make damn sure he doesn't make any more."

Tightening her hold on him, she pressed her cheek against his. "You and I..." she whispered. "You and I are going to be very happy together."

Outside on the long runway, the plane to California sped along the tarmac, then lifted slowly into the sky. Both D.B. and Margo turned their heads to see its blinking lights bank into a turn and head into the western sky.

"Looks like I won't be going to California tonight after all," she said dreamily.

"No. We're going back to the ranch," he said with a purr of satisfaction. "I think we should use the rest of your vacation for a honeymoon. We'll call George from there and let him and Grace know what's going on."

Her eyes sparkled up at his. "A honeymoon, huh? What will everyone think?"

He laughed. "Wanda already thinks I'm sleeping with you. And the twins are counting on me to bring you back."

She laughed, too, then kissed him—slowly, provocatively and lovingly. "Then we'd better hit the road," she whispered against his lips. "I don't want anyone to be disappointed. Especially not you, my love."

Epilogue

Margo paused on the threshold leading into the plushly furnished office. Her husband was working at a wide mahogany desk, dark glasses and a look of deep concentration on his face. The loden green tie at his throat matched the pinstripes in his starched dress shirt and the jade cuff links at his wrists were the ones Margo had given him as a gift. Not a special occasion gift, but simply as an "I love you" gift.

He looked every inch the handsome, powerful businessman, until he spotted her and rose to his feet. Then she smiled affectionately as she took in his blue jeans, wide leather belt and Western boots. This other half of him was her sexy, macho cowboy.

"Hello, darling," D.B. told her as he came around the desk and took his wife into his arms. "What are you doing down here at the office? I thought you and Emily were going shopping today."

Margo raised up on tiptoe and kissed him. "We did. I wanted to come by and show you what I got for our daughter to wear on the ranch. It's the cutest little hat you've ever seen. One of those felt ones with the white stitching around the brim and a stampede string to draw up under her chin."

D.B. laughed at the thought of their rambunctious ten-month-old daughter keeping a hat on her head for more than five minutes. "Sounds like she's all set to ride the range. How about you? Got most of our things packed?"

Margo nodded excitedly. It was spring and they were leaving for the Silver Spur tonight. She and D.B. had been married for nearly two years now, and the months they spent on the ranch together were cherished and eagerly awaited.

However, she could also say that their life here in California was cherished, too. She was still working as head legal adviser for Barlow and Associates, although, since Emily had been born, she'd drastically cut her working hours at the office. D.B. had made peace with his father, and George finally understood he had to step back and give his son breathing room. Because of it, D.B. could finally enjoy working at the Barlow brokerage firm. Even so, Margo knew her husband needed his time at the Silver Spur and she was always going to make sure he got it.

"I know you're going to say I've packed too much," Margo told him. "But Emily is so messy. And Wanda and I don't want to spend all of our time at the washing machine."

Smiling at her, he shook his head. "Oh, you'd rather be cooking?"

She gouged him in the ribs with her finger. "You know I'd rather be riding. Ringo has missed me."

His brown eyes full of love, he said, "No doubt he has. I certainly couldn't do without you for six months. In fact, I don't want to do without you for six minutes."

Bending his head, his lips hovered just above hers. "Speaking of six minutes. Where is our daughter now?"

Her hands tightened on his shoulders as she anticipated his kiss. "With your father. He's showing her the boardroom."

"Again? He's showed her the boardroom at least twenty times," D.B. said with wry fondness.

Margo chuckled. "I know. He just can't wait until she gets old enough to be a businesswoman."

D.B. brushed his lips teasingly against Margo's. "And I can't wait until she gets old enough to be a cowgirl."

Margo sighed. "I hope you two aren't going to fight over Emily."

D.B. laughed. "Not a chance. Hopefully my daughter is going to have the best of both worlds. Just like me."

He kissed her then, long and lingering. Afterward, Margo looked up at him dreamily. "And what about your son?"

His dark brows arched in a hopeful question. "My son? Are you pregnant again?"

Laughing throatily, she slid her arms around his waist. "I'm sure I will be before we leave the ranch. After all, what's a couple to do with all that quiet solitude on their hands?"

"Mmm," he purred, his arms tightening around her. "If that's what you have in mind, it's a good thing I'm putting the twins to work this spring as regular ranch hands. Otherwise, we might not have any time to ourselves."

Margo laughed. "You know how much the twins look forward to spending the summer with us. And to tell you the truth, I'd be disappointed if they didn't. They're like family now."

He rubbed his cheek against hers. "And they always will be. They made me realize how much I loved you and urged me to go after you."

"Smart boys," Margo said, turning her head to seek out his lips once again. At the same moment, George strolled into the office carrying a dark-haired baby with a red cowboy hat perched on one side of her little head.

"All right, none of that during business hours," George scolded jokingly.

Both D.B. and Margo turned toward the older man, who appeared to be fit as a fiddle now that the doctors had discovered the problem with his heart and were treating him with the right medication.

Emily reached for her daddy. D.B. took the baby from George and kissed her fat little cheek. "Are you ready to go ride a horse, Emmy?"

While D.B. was cooing over his daughter, Margo turned to George. "Are you coming up to the ranch, George? The snow should be cleared out in about three weeks."

"I'm looking forward to it," the older man said, then turned toward his son. "Now that you've shown me what a success this dude ranch of yours is, D.B., I've got a proposition for you."

Both Margo and D.B. groaned.

"Please, Dad, no propositions," D.B. told him. "We like the ranch just as it is."

"But if you bulldozed those rickety old cabins down and built new ones—"

"We'd lose the authenticity of the place, and that's one of the reasons the guests come back year after year."

"But I've already written you a check to make improvements," George insisted.

D.B. exchanged a knowing glance with his wife. George was once again trying to tell his son he loved him. Thankfully, this time D.B. understood all that.

"Good. I'll accept the check and start Emily a new herd of Angus. By the time she's grown, she'll have a fortune in cattle."

For a moment George looked taken aback and looked as if he wanted to argue the point. But then suddenly he laughed and reached in his pocket for the folded check.

With a wink at Margo, he said proudly, "That's my son."

Margo smiled. George was finally learning what loving was all about.

*   *   *   *   *

It's our 1000th
Silhouette Romance
and we're celebrating!

Join us for a special collection of love stories by the authors you've loved for years, and new favorites you've just discovered.

**It's a celebration just for you,
with wonderful books by
Diana Palmer, Suzanne Carey,
Tracy Sinclair, Marie Ferrarella,
Debbie Macomber, Laurie Paige,
Annette Broadrick, Elizabeth August
and MORE!**

Silhouette Romance...vibrant, fun and emotionally rich! Take another look at us!

As part of the celebration, readers can receive a FREE gift AND enter our exciting sweepstakes to win a grand prize of $1000! Look for more details in all March Silhouette series titles.

**You'll fall in love all over again
with Silhouette Romance!**

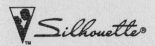

CEL1000T

Take 4 bestselling love stories FREE

Plus get a FREE surprise gift!

Special Limited-time Offer

Mail to Silhouette Reader Service™

3010 Walden Avenue
P.O. Box 1867
Buffalo, N.Y. 14269-1867

YES! Please send me 4 free Silhouette Romance™ novels and my free surprise gift. Then send me 6 brand-new novels every month, which I will receive months before they appear in bookstores. Bill me at the low price of $2.19 each plus 25¢ delivery and applicable sales tax, if any.* That's the complete price and—compared to the cover prices of $2.75 each—quite a bargain! I understand that accepting the books and gift places me under no obligation ever to buy any books. I can always return a shipment and cancel at any time. Even if I never buy another book from Silhouette, the 4 free books and the surprise gift are mine to keep forever.

215 BPA ANRP

Name	(PLEASE PRINT)	
Address	Apt. No.	
City	State	Zip

This offer is limited to one order per household and not valid to present Silhouette Romance™ subscribers. *Terms and prices are subject to change without notice. Sales tax applicable in N.Y.

USROM-94R   ©1990 Harlequin Enterprises Limited

HE'S MORE THAN A MAN, HE'S ONE OF OUR

Fabulous Fathers

CALEB'S SON
by Laurie Paige

Handsome widower Caleb Remmick had a business to run and a son to raise—alone. Finding help wasn't easy—especially when the only one offering was Eden Sommers. Years ago he'd asked for her hand, but Eden refused to live with his workaholic ways. Now his son, Josh, needed someone, and Eden was the only woman he'd ever trust—and the only woman he'd ever loved....

Look for *Caleb's Son* by Laurie Paige, available in March.

Fall in love with our Fabulous Fathers!

Silhouette
ROMANCE™

FF394

**And now for
something completely different
from Silhouette....**

SPELLBOUND
R O M A N C E

Unique and innovative stories that take you into the world of paranormal happenings. Look for our special "Spellbound" flash—and get ready for a truly exciting reading experience!

**In February, look for
One Unbelievable Man (SR #993)
by Pat Montana.**

Was he man or myth? Cass Kohlmann's mysterious traveling companion, Michael O'Shea, had her all confused. He'd suddenly appeared, claiming she was his destiny—determined to win her heart. But could levelheaded Cass learn to believe in fairy tales...before her fantasy man disappeared forever?

Don't miss the charming, sexy and utterly mysterious
Michael O'Shea in
ONE UNBELIEVABLE MAN.
Watch for him in February—only from

Silhouette
R O M A N C E™

SPELL2

As seen on TV!
Free Gift Offer

With a Free Gift proof-of-purchase from any Silhouette® book,
you can receive a beautiful cubic zirconia pendant.

This gorgeous marquise-shaped stone is a genuine cubic
zirconia—accented by an 18" gold tone necklace.
(Approximate retail value $19.95)

Send for yours today...
compliments of ▼ *Silhouette*®

To receive your free gift, a cubic zirconia pendant, send us one original proof-of-
purchase, photocopies not accepted, from the back of any Silhouette Romance™,
Silhouette Desire®, Silhouette Special Edition®, Silhouette Intimate Moments® or
Silhouette Shadows™ title for January, February or March 1994 at your favorite retail
outlet, together with the Free Gift Certificate, plus a check or money order for $2.50
(do not send cash) to cover postage and handling, payable to Silhouette Free Gift Offer.
We will send you the specified gift. Allow 6 to 8 weeks for delivery. Offer good until
March 31st, 1994 or while quantities last. Offer valid in the U.S. and Canada only.

Free Gift Certificate

Name: _____

Address: _____

City: _____ State/Province: _____ Zip/Postal Code: _____

Mail this certificate, one proof-of-purchase and a check or money order for postage
and handling to: SILHOUETTE FREE GIFT OFFER 1994. In the U.S.: 3010 Walden
Avenue, P.O. Box 9057, Buffalo NY 14269-9057. In Canada: P.O. Box 622, Fort Erie,
Ontario L2Z 5X3

FREE GIFT OFFER   079-KBZ
ONE PROOF-OF-PURCHASE
To collect your fabulous FREE GIFT, a cubic zirconia pendant, you must include this
original proof-of-purchase for each gift with the properly completed Free Gift Certificate.

079-KBZ